Heather Hughes-Calero

THE SEDONA TRILOGY

Book Three

Land of Nome

Presented with love . . . in SUGMAD

D1446238

Coastline Publishing Company
California

1985

9/98

THE SEDONA TRILOGY

Book Three *The Land of Nome*
by Heather Hughes-Calero

COASTLINE PUBLISHING COMPANY
Post Office Box 223062
Carmel, California 93922

Copyright ©1985 Heather Hughes-Calero
Second Printing 1987
Printed in the United States of America

Cover by Lois Stanfield.

Library of Congress Catalog No. 85-89058
ISBN: 0-932927-02-5

Gift
Sale

To W A H - Z

CHAPTER 1

The old messenger stood in the doorway, leaning upon his walking stick, gazing firmly at Deetra.

Deetra knew he was there, yet she did not raise her head, but remained bent over her work table, studying some scrolls a scribe had sent her.

It was not unusual for the old messenger to be gazing at her. Since her return from the causal plane with the Chief Elder Sarpent, the messenger seemed always to be near her. And there seemed to be little purpose to his visitations. He projected no thoughts of urgency or concern and seldom did he speak. When he did, it was in phrases like "May the blessings Be!" or "Be with SUGMAD!" She would glance up and answer him in like phrase and then return to her work. And following this, he stood silent and watched her while she went about her business and then, when next she would look up, he would be gone.

This time the old messenger did not announce himself in greeting, but stood motionless, watching her.

There was something intense about his presence this day and Deetra could not ignore him. The old messenger was outwardly silent but not inwardly. She raised her head and turned to him. "Be with SUGMAD!" she said, greeting him.

"Be with SUGMAD!" the messenger repeated.

"Has my husband Lord Ian sent word for me?" she asked.

"No, he has not, but I am told that he will return to

the sanctuary before the new moon," the old messenger said slowly.

What the old man said was not news to Deetra. It was the time Ian had said he would return. She looked away briefly, thoughtfully. The intensity of the old man's presence seemed to pull at her.

What did he wish?

She started to ask, turning to him once again, but the old man was gone.

He seemed to disappear the moment she placed her full attention on him.

But why?

He had obviously wanted her attention.

For a long moment she stood looking into the empty doorway where the old messenger had been, recalling the first time she had seen him. He had been an attendant of the Ancient One prior to Awakening Day, and it was he who had handed her the crystal, a gift from the Hanta to use as a tool to journey to the City of Light. It was also the old messenger who called her to the sanctuary for her marriage to Ian, and it was he who had led her to the iron gate which led to a meeting with Ian, transfigured as Hanta. Now Ian was not only her husband but he was the Hanta, the Holy One. She would never forget the impact of that discovery.

And it was also the old messenger who gave her student Tolar his crystal. She had witnessed the scene with the adept Ramus-i-Rabriz from the causal plane, through a doorway between the worlds.

The old messenger's role was unlike most servants, the fulfillment of his duty often uplifted a moment to greatness. He seemed a humble person, yet he had the countenance of a spiritual adept. It was plainly seen that he was no ordinary servant.

Why had she not thought on it before now?

A memory of the old messenger crept forward in her

mind. He had arrived at her father's house to summon her to the sanctuary to prepare for her marriage to Ian. She had questioned him as to the urgency of her leave and as she had done so, she recalled the overlapping images of the Hanta and Ian. The images had seemed to be more pronounced than the mental images one carries from another's thoughts.

What did it mean?

Her skin prickled at the memory and she quickly dismissed it. The past was not the point. It was the present that was in issue. There was some reason the old messenger was ever-present in her daily affairs. Perhaps Ian had asked him to keep watch over her.

But why?

Keep watch over her from what?

To protect her?

It was absurd.

She was an awakened spiritual being. She had no need of anyone to be watchful over her ... unless ...

She stopped. Raising herself from the work table, she walked slowly over to the window and looked out. It was still early and the morning dew had not yet dried on the trees outside her window. She could see the wetness on the leaves, shining in the bright sunrise.

Was she deceiving herself?

Since Ian, as Hanta, had journeyed out to visit the people of neighboring villages, she had spent almost every moment in study. Was she somehow missing the point in her studies? Did her actions and thoughts betray this fact in some way?

Inwardly, she examined her behavior, seeing herself on the mental screen and watching herself. It was Soul who was the watcher.

If she was somehow missing the finer points in her studies she would in time learn what it was that she was missing. The scrolls seemed to open up in meaning a little more each time she read them.

Why then had she considered deceiving herself?

What did it matter?

There was no way she could hang onto deceit for long if it were true.

Her skin prickled again and for an instant she was back on the causal plane with Sarpent, trying to encourage the Chief Elder to break free from his bonds of illusion.

Was she, herself, in that danger?

The answer was not long in coming. She was always in that danger just as anyone else endeavoring to live in a higher state of consciousness.

Was that why the old messenger visited her so often?

It occurred to her that perhaps he was looking for assistance and was hesitant to ask but she quickly dismissed the idea. From the attention being shown her, there was no doubt that his presence was intended for her benefit.

For what reason?

As if the question has been spoken aloud in demand of answer, she turned from the window, facing the interior of her tiny study room. She hesitated, then reached for the scroll on her work table and began to read aloud:

Does space, when measured by distance, have an effect on thought?

The question is one of psychic perception and both of consequence and little consequence to the student of lower plane law, because it both does and it doesn't. The astral or emotional consciousness can easily be disturbed by space to the one who is unaware, however to the one functioning on a higher level of consciousness, the overview of such would not permit such indulgence.

She returned the parchment to her work table, recalling how she had pondered on the question and answer. It was one of many she had dealt with in her studies and she had felt it quite interesting to challenge herself. It was the part of her training which assisted in filling in the gaps of her knowledge of the mental planes and she greatly enjoyed it.

That was it!

The realization struck her like a bolt of lightening. It was not that she was deceiving herself by neglecting her training, but by indulging in the mental gymnastics of the mind plane. She was enjoying the sport to an extreme in that she was spending all of her time toying with it. Here it was still early morning and she had already been working for hours.

There had to be balance.

Suddenly she looked up to the doorway where the old messenger had been standing, half expecting to see him there, but he wasn't. Yet the doorway appeared inviting. She would spend the day refreshing herself; enjoy a walk in the open air; perhaps a visit to the marketplace where she would mingle among the villagers.

It was a glorious morning. The sun peeking in and out of thick milk white clouds interspersed with patches of deep blue sky. The air was warm and just a faint trickle of a cool breeze reminded her that it was not yet summer. She had been married to Ian for nearly three years; three years that had been a lifetime of experiences for the average person, but then the experiences could not be called average.

In those three years she had experienced the inner world of the causal and mental planes; had travelled the time track of incarnations; had wrestled with the secrets of quieting minds and had broken free from the chains of outward appearances. She no longer had thoughts or desire for the material world. They had been replaced with a deep longing for the divine source—for the SUGMAD. If it were not for Ian there would be no holding her to the physical plane. She would have voluntarily translated into the planes of Soul, but Ian needed her—not in the conventional sense but rather cherished her as a partner in life. And she needed him in this way too.

But there was little time together.

Ian had accepted the mantle of power. He was the Hanta, the Holy One, the Godman. It was his task to lead all who would follow to the great moment of Awakening Day. The task was enormous, lifting the karmic burdens of so many in order to help them gain their spiritual legs. And then he had the delicate task of educating and guiding them through the unseen worlds and then returning the karmic burdens to their rightful heirs at a time when he felt the individual to be strong enough to bear them. Then and only then did the Hanta stand back and let the individuals fend for themselves. But there were always many to work with, and as Hanta he would never be without duty to perform.

Deetra thought of her husband now, travelling from village to village, meeting with the people and answering their questions. As wife to this great being, what was she contributing?

Indeed what was her role?

Until now it seemed small. She had served through teaching a class on spiritual law and learning the answers to her own questions while adventuring on the inbetween planes. Now it seemed she was merely reviewing, testing herself at what she already knew.

It was true.

She had no more questions. Everything that she had once ached to know had been answered. Now she was learning from another level. She was learning that which she had never had the consciousness to question; that which she did not even know existed. Her training in the lower worlds was finished. She was now working purely in the areas of Soul.

She paused on the road, allowing the realization to linger. Never had she realized such happiness as she had known of late. It was an inner happiness not dependent on the outside world. It was perfect, harmonious, loving and giving.

And yet she knew.

She had to give more.

Being a channel for the Divine Force demanded an outgoing nature. Of late, she had isolated herself to study and the results she knew were lacking. She was focusing too much on self, whereby she needed to be out among the people and as a channel to touch them in some way by merely being with them. She was a carrier of the Divine Force. Wherever she placed her attention was touched by that Force and of late the touching was indulgent of self.

The marketplace was alive with chatter and movement and as Deetra approached she stood still a moment, looking about and then entered.

She recognized and greeted almost everyone she passed. She had grown up with these people, had known them since childhood. They were the villagers of her village and she was one of them, yet they all knew that it was not true. Deetra once lived in the village but now she was not of it. The villagers sensed it as she did. She was Askan, an awakened one and they stood in awe of her, friendly but distant. She was not of their inner circle, nor could she pretend to be.

But that was not always so.

There was a time before she had entered the City of Light that she was one of them, believing the Askan to be some supernatural being who could change the countenance of the mountains and walk in mid-air. The Askan were feared because they were not understood and out of this ignorance superstition sprung.

It was ridiculous.

She was not a supernatural being, nor was Sarpent the Chief Elder, nor Rian the Scribe or her father Starn or Ian. She hesitated in thought. Ian was a supernatural being. As

Hanta he was the Great One—omnipresent, omnipotent, and omniscient; and in like manner all Askan were to some degree supernatural. They were aware of Soul and of the illusions of the lower worlds and therefore lived freely, without limitations. It was why they could be in the village and yet not of it. They were the channels for the Divine Force, silently igniting the flame of Soul in those they contacted.

Today in the marketplace she was a channel.

She stopped to examine a silky piece of pale yellow cloth. It was beautiful in texture as well as color and there was a soft sheen to it that caught her fancy. She asked the proprietor the price.

The figure in the market stall had his back to her and as he turned, he slowly raised his head. His eyes met Deetra's.

A slow chill ran through Deetra and she was too astonished to speak. The man before her was the weak frame of an elderly man she did not recognize, yet there was something in the face, most particularly in the eyes, which she did. And the eyes which looked back at her seemed to know her as well.

Neither spoke, but in the silence there was imagery and the imagery told the story of confronting the being before her in many other guises. The image smiled at the recognition. It was the Pink Prince. It was Lord Casmir. In composite, it was the negative force.

But why?

Although he seemed ever-present as a force in her physical life, she had not seen him personified since her journey to the East with Sarpent when she had seen him through the doorways between the worlds.

Why was he confronting her now?

What had she done to draw him to her?

The merchant held up the cloth she had been admiring. "It is yours as a gift," he said. "It is the least I can give to the Lady Deetra."

Deetra stood staring at the man as though hypnotised. It was as if all else was shut out and, except for the sound of his voice, there was total silence. No longer did she hear the other merchants and villagers. It was as though they had faded into the distant background.

"It will look exquisite on you," the merchant said to her again. "And each time you wear it you will remember that it was given to you by an admirer."

Deetra heard the words and for an instant recalled her initial astonishment of recognizing a glimmer in the old merchant's face. Had she been mistaken?

"Yes, yes," the merchant said. "It is meant for you, and such an honor it is to be the giver of such a gift. You honor me lady in accepting it." He held it out to her again, this time draping it about one of her shoulders.

A thin wisp of a breeze moved past her, and its movement caught her attention. In it was a faint sound she had grown to love and trust, the hum of the wind, HUuuuu. It was without and about her, but it was within her as well.

She brushed the yellow cloth from her shoulders and handed it back to the merchant. Withdrawing her eyes from him she said, "Thank you very much!" Then she turned and walked away.

Her attention was instantly drawn. Just ahead a small crowd of people gathered. They were looking at something and talking excitedly. Deetra went over to see what it was.

On a table in front of the people was a miniature village much like their own, and in it there were people, little people about six inches high, walking about the marketplace. Looking closer she saw that a group of little people were standing, peering over each other's heads, looking at a display table. The display itself could not be seen. It was in looking for it that Deetra realized that she was seeing tiny images of herself and those who stood looking with her. Quickly she turned and looked around. To the left and right were reflective devices and colored lights and these had formed the illusion of the miniature village, utilizing those curious people present to be the actors. Then she saw the person responsible for the display. She didn't notice him at first because he appeared to be one of the watchers. His manipulations were only visible within the miniature gathering. There he could be seen doing all sorts of trickery— waving his arms to accentuate motion within the scene and still not attract undue attention to himself. What was happening was he was animating a scene so peculiar that no one noticed his involvement. As she recognized what was taking place, she moved back a few steps, out of range of the projector which reflected the images and she stood looking at the operator.

"You can't leave that easily," he called after her without turning around. "You have a responsibility to these people. They do not know that they are within my powers."

Deetra knew without the operator's turning around who it was. She shuddered, wondering why the negative force was so conscious of her this day. She said nothing, but turned and left the arena.

In that moment she wanted to be out of the marketplace, but instead she was in the heart of it. There was no time to be singularly alone now except to inwardly sing the HU and to listen within for that thin high-pitched sound which would come forward from Soul. She knew she must not get caught in thought nor try to analyze the cirmcumstances of the events she had just witnessed. She had to keep her wits about her.

Then she saw the most astonishing thing.

Every person she saw at the market bore the mark of the negative force. In each and every person she saw the expression of Lord Casmir or the Pink Prince, and each greeted her kindly as if she was some attracting entity. What was happening?

Had she slipped from consciousness?

Was she asleep in some nightmare state?

She had left her work at the sanctuary to spend time among the villagers as a channel for the Divine Force. She had expected to function as CAUSE but instead she had become the EFFECT. What had happened?

The answer came slowly. It rose from deep within herself and surfaced in surprise. She had left the sanctuary in an analytical state and had entered the daily lives of the villagers, carrying with her all of the mental symbolism she had been studying. In turn, she realized quite suddenly that she had projected her state of consciousness into those around her. It was a state of consciousness which had been reviewing the psychic worlds—the realm of the negative force.

She lowered her eyes so as not to interlock with passersby and continued to walk slowly, softly singing the sound of HU as she passed. She continued on this way for what seemed quite a long time until someone touched her on the shoulder. She stopped and spun around.

The old messenger stood before her, gazing silently while she inwardly composed herself.

What was he doing here?

Had he followed her?

"I felt you might need some assistance with your packages but I see that you have acquired none," the old messenger said.

"No, none," Deetra said, uncertain.

"I saw you receiving a yellow cloth," he said smiling, "but I see I was mistaken."

"Yes, you were mistaken," Deetra said. "It was given to me but I did not accept it."

"I see."

Deetra was suddenly annoyed at the discovery that she had been spied upon.

"And what of the responsibility you had to the wee people of the miniature village?" the old messenger asked.

[*13*]

"I had no responsibility," she said, controlling the tone of her voice.

"I see," the old man said again.

"You see? What is it you see, old man?" She looked away for a moment and motioned to the marketplace with a sweep of her hand. When she turned back to the old messenger again, he was not there.

He had gone.

But where?

Looking about, she recalled earlier in the morning when she had looked up from her work to greet the old man and he had suddenly disappeared. She remembered how intense she believed he had been; how because of his disturbing presence she had come to realize her own overworked, imbalanced situation and had decided to spend the day outdoors. And now she saw that she had not left her imbalanced situation behind but had taken it with her and had entered the village marketplace as EFFECT rather than CAUSE. She had created the strange happenings through an aberrated viewpoint. It was true, but she had not created the appearance of the old messenger.

CHAPTER 2

In the days that followed, Deetra spent less time with her work and more time outdoors, relaxing lazily on the sanctuary lawn just outside her chamber. And during that time she did not see the old messenger, nor was she subjected to any out of the way happenings. It was a quiet, recuperative time for her and she enjoyed the contrasting feeling of the warm sun against the cool grass where she reclined.

There was much to consider and she needed the time to think and to contemplate. She wanted to be more outwardly constructive; to function in the world in some way; to reach down into the depths of herself and to give creatively as an inspired channel for the Divine Force. She needed to serve the Hanta consciousness, for the sake of that consciousness and for the sake of her own.

But how?

In what way was she best equipped to give of herself?

It wasn't until the third day that she had realized the answer. She shouldn't have been surprised but she was and the surprise delighted her because the solution was so natural, so simple that she should have known it without undue thought.

She need only move among the people and speak about the Force and the indwelling element of it within each of them. She would do this in a special way, as a spiritual law class only it would be more open, inviting everyone to attend, not just those seekers who would normally come.

She would give them a basic introduction into the meaning of the Force, and understanding of the Askan, and seek to dispel the myths, superstition and ignorance that had been built up over the centuries. In dispelling fears spawned through ignorance, it may be that there would be many more ready to seek the City of Light than those who have already shown themselves.

She would get to work.

With this conclusion, she automatically rose to her feet, and a feeling of excitement rushed through her. She did not know where she would begin or how, but she would begin.

The marketplace was as she remembered it in that everyone was busy and engaged in the fine art of bartering, and the sun was shining, but different in that there was a lightness to the mood of the people. She knew this was because she was seeing them in this way. And she wasn't there to be idle among them. She had work to do and she was prepared to do it.

She had brought with her six pieces of parchment on which she had written her intentions, inviting those interested to participate. On each it read:

Hear what you always wanted to know
about . . . Askan,
The City of Light,
Your True Identity
Everyone invited
Village Square, Daily at Noon.

She posted the notices throughout the marketplace, chatting with curious passersby and then hurriedly returned to the sanctuary, filled with a feeling of joy and excitement. Tomorrow she would set out for the Village Square to begin.

The next day she arrived at the Village Square shortly

before noon. The stone benches encircling the inside of the square were perfect for informal discussion and she did wish the talk to be informal, where everyone would have the feeling of participation. As she stood in the center of the circle thinking on these things, a number of people passed by, nodding a courteous greeting, continuing on their way. She knew they were curious, possibly wanting to attend the talk but not wishing to draw attention to themselves nor to be the first to arrive. Friendliness or inviting them did not seem to be the answer. Gradually she became aware that when she was not paying direct attention to a passing person that he lingered, as if more at ease, waiting to see what was to take place. Noticing this, she chose a stone bench and sat down, withdrawing a parchment from the folds of her gown and began to read.

Man in his ordinary state is a machine. He functions automatically without conscious recognition of his true identity. Indeed he has little or no knowledge of self at all. He eats when he gets hungry and he cries when he feels pain. He is bound to emotions and is enslaved by his mind. He carries with him all the fears and aberrations impressed upon him in his childhood, many of which have been carried forward from childhood to childhood as he passed from incarnation to incarnation. He has made symbols of important figures in his life and becomes aberrated by the symbols. Thus, he walks about blindly, knowing full well that there must be more to the heights of life until, through his seeking, he is finally accepted by the Hanta and begins the difficult journey to the City of Light, finally becoming Askan, journeying to the SUGMAD.

Deetra had become lost in the scroll, not so much in its message but in seeking inner guidance as to how to make the message understood to those who would meet with her.

It would be useless to give each a copy of the scroll unless the individual was ready to begin the journey to the City of Light. She must find some simple way of making herself understood.

Thoughtfully glancing up, she was pleasantly surprised. All of the benches were filled, except one where some objects had been placed as if to save the space, and no one had sat next to her. It was not a large gathering but a substantial one, fifteen in all and looking from face to face she knew everyone, although some better than others. And there was one other Askan, her father Starn. She smiled in greeting, silently noting that he had seen her notice in the marketplace and was there as a supporting channel. And there was also Tolar who, although not yet Askan, had begun his inward journey to the City of Light. He was a student of her spiritual law class and an apt student. She welcomed him warmly. The others present were not those she had taught before but rather they were the villagers she sought to reach. They were the curious and she knew that it was in reaching out that the path of awareness began.

"You are all welcome," she said warmly. "This is the first of an everyday meeting to be held here. Many of you will not find it possible to come every day but that matters little. Come as it is timely for you to come, and bring a friend if you like." She paused, searching for a beginning. "I have promised you explanations," she said, hesitating.

"Yes, you have," a bearded man called from a bench across from her. It was the village doctor. "And I hope we are going to get some direct answers."

"That is my purpose," Deetra said, "but sometimes directness requires prior explanation. You cannot explain a disease without discussion on its causes as well as its effects."

The physician laughed. "Knowing the cause of a disease is wishful thinking," he said, "therefore it is only the effects with which we concern ourselves."

[*18*]

"But in treating effects, the disease will return," Deetra said.

"Mostly yes," the physician said, hesitantly. "but the cause of a disease is a mystery locked within the individual."

"Then we will begin in this way," Deetra said, thinking aloud. "I have wondered how to begin explanation and now the doctor has given us the answer.

"One of the answers I have promised you is what makes an Askan. The answer is that the Askan knows himself. There are no mysteries for the Askan. He need only use spiritual eyes to look within to solve the riddles of self."

"You mean you know the cause for everything?" a woman sitting near the doctor asked.

"I mean the tools are at hand," Deetra said.

"And is that a direct answer," the physician asked. He folded his arms across his chest and swayed side to side on his seat.

"Indeed it is a direct answer," Deetra said. "An Askan knows himself. He knows that all answers are attached to the question. He knows that to draw forth any knowledge he need only look within. But the Askan is also a human being and as such undergoes trials and tribulations such as anyone else. In difficult times he may be at a loss for answers. But the remedy is close at hand and he knows it. He need only detach his feelings from the difficulty and he will soar above it, free."

"You make it sound so simple," the woman said.

Deetra nodded. "It is simple," she said, "but it is not always easy."

"What of the City of Light?" someone called out.

Deetra's attention went to Tolar who was sitting quietly off to the side. "Perhaps someone undertaking that journey now would like to speak of it," she said.

Tolar sat erect and shook his head. "I do not know what to say," he said.

She waited, her attention still on Tolar.

"It is nothing as you would imagine," Tolar said uncomfortably.

"In what way?" Deetra asked.

"It is not physical," he said, "and yet it is. It's a journey into an invisible world but the physical world reflects it."

"Meaning?" Deetra asked, prodding.

"Something like 'as above, so below,'" Tolar said, "but one is not up and the other down."

"Why is that?" she asked him again.

Tolar hesitated thoughtfully. "I'm not certain," he said.

"It is because what we are talking about is outside of time and space," Deetra said. "The City of Light is not trapped within this dimension, however its reflection is." She paused, looking from face to face. The perplexion was obvious. The physician had unfolded his arms but was now gripping the seat of the bench with his hands.

"What all this means," Deetra said, "is that the physical world is a reflection of the invisible. Within the invisible is the City of Light. In order to enter one must be aware of one's true identity."

"Which brings us to the third item on your notice," the physician said.

"The true identity is Soul," Deetra said.

"Which is?" the physician asked.

"Spirit," Deetra said.

"Which is?" he asked again.

"The Divine Force," Deetra said.

"In what way?" he asked.

"In all ways," she said.

There was a moment of silence. Suddenly the physician rose from his seat. "I have matters I must attend to but I regret that I have to leave. You will be here tomorrow?" he asked.

"Yes, at noon," Deetra said.

"And can we talk at greater length on these subjects?"

he asked.

"Yes, we can," she said, smiling, pleased that his gruffness had meant interest in learning more. "We can discuss any number of things."

The physician nodded and then turned and left the square.

Deetra turned her attention to the others. "I hope that you have all gotten something from this discussion. It will be all for today. Thank you for coming," she said and rose from her seat.

Starn approached her and gave her a hug. "This is an interesting plan of yours my daughter," he said, "and I have another reason for attending."

She looked closely at her father but his feelings did not project thought.

"I'm off to join the Hanta's caravan," he said seriously.

"Ian has sent for you?" she asked.

"No," Starn said seriously. "He did not send for me but the urge to attend him is great."

Deetra studied the firm lines of her father's face. They were lines etched from living with a purpose and she understood. She too had come to realize that she must give fully in order to know joy.

"Have you heard of Ian's location?" Deetra asked.

"I'm sure I'll find him without much trouble," Starn said, smiling. "And the adventures along the way will surely prove valuable in preparing me for the reunion."

"I envy you," she said lightly.

"It seems you have found your own way," Starn said, motioning to the small gathering about them. "And, my daughter, I see it as a grand idea."

"When do you leave?" she asked.

"I am ready to depart now," he said. "It is my plan to leave from here. As you can see my supplies are ready." He motioned to the stone bench that had items stacked on one end. "Our neighbor is to meet me here with a burro and then I leave."

She eyed his belongings, sighing lightly. "I have not seen you much lately but I shall miss you anyway," she said.

He laughed. "Then perhaps you'll take some time and talk with me along the way," he said.

She smiled in return, knowing full well what her father meant. They had only to communicate in thought at any time to be together. Yet she had been too preoccupied of late to do this. He was asking her to tune in to him on occasion.

A tall, thin man appeared on the north side of the square. With him was the burro her father was waiting to receive. Starn waved to him, acknowledging his presence.

"Well, my daughter, my love surrounds you," Starn said, drawing her near. "I will return with your husband."

Deetra hugged her father tightly and then released him. "May your adventures be joyful," she said lovingly. "And should you wish a friend, you need only call on me."

"Thank you my daughter," Starn said. "And now it is time that I leave." He stepped back from her and blew her a kiss, then waved and turned on his heels.

Deetra watched as he disappeared from the square and then turned about. Everyone had left except for Tolar and he waited until she had seen him and then he approached.

"May I walk you to the sanctuary?" he asked.

"Of course," she said, "I would be delighted."

They walked on silently for a few moments. The warm afternoon sun beat down on them. Deetra remembered a time well over a year ago when Tolar had asked to walk her to her father's house. It was after a spiritual law class and he had been seeking the Hanta and a way to the City of Light. He had found the way now and was a crystal bearer. She remembered seeing him receive that crystal from the old messenger as she stood with the great spiritual adept of the causal plane, looking through the doorways between the worlds. She had felt great love and compassion for the student then as she did now.

"I want to thank you," Tolar said.

"You have nothing to thank me for," Deetra said.

"But you have helped me in so many ways, sometimes by just a reassuring glance," Tolar said.

"I am glad," she said, "and it was my privilege. You will learn that there is no greater joy than serving the force."

"That's what I wanted to ask you," Tolar said.

She turned to face him as they continued walking.

"I want to know how I can serve," he said.

She looked away. "When it is time, you will know," she said. "There is no way to rush the readiness. Meanwhile you are serving by preparing, you are filling yourself. I see you as a lovely channel." She turned to him again and smiled.

"Thank you ... thank you," he said.

They were silent again although Deetra could hear that the man was suffering from a rushing stream of thought. She did not try to listen to it. As they rounded the bend, the sanctuary came into view. Suddenly Tolar jumped out front and stood bravely before her.

She stopped, staring at the older man. There was an air of urgency about him. He was trying to collect himself to speak.

"Yes," she said, encouraging him. "You have something you wish to tell me."

"There is a caller," he said anxiously. "Every day a woman arrives at my house. She reminds me of my departed wife, only this woman says luring things to me. I have the feeling that she is trying to trap me in some way."

"You are still an attractive man, Tolar," Deetra said, studying the interesting lines of the older man's face. He was middle-aged with a full head of wavy white hair.

"That's not what I mean," he said. "There's something about the woman that is not a woman at all. Sometimes when I turn my head a certain way, I see a man and not a woman. Whatever, to me it is not a man or a woman. It is a being of some sort and it does not intend to treat me well."

Deetra looked long and deeply into the man's face. She realized the earnestness of his feelings and the sincerity of what he felt. He was deeply troubled by the presence of his visitor. "How long has this been going on?" she asked.

"Weeks! Every day at the same time the woman is there. And if I am not home when she arrives, she leaves a calling gift," he said.

"What sort of a calling gift?" Deetra asked.

"It's always a jewel," he said anxiously, "a jewel or a piece of glass and it's always pink."

Deetra drew in a long breath.

"You know what it is?" he asked.

As Tolar had been telling her his story, she had seen the image of the negative force approaching the man. She had experienced it so many times herself, only it came to her in different forms. The pink jewels he had received as a gift confirmed her knowingness. "You are on Moonwalk," she said softly.

Tolar stared at her, the blood rushing through his veins. It sounded as though drums pounded in his ears. He had heard tales of Moonwalk from the villagers. All his life he had heard these tales, just as he had heard tales of the Askan and their supernatural powers. It was said that in order to be Askan, one had to pass through the terrible Moonwalk, and that many died along the way.

Deetra heard the panic of his thoughts and the compassion she had once felt for this man now deepened. She too had travelled Moonwalk and she remembered the great trial and tribulations she had encountered there. It was where one came face to face with the negative force. It was the first circle within the inner circle and only the bold and daring could survive. "I feel confident you will make it," Deetra said, reassuringly.

The man now looked like a boy and a very frightened

one.

"Practice the presence of the Hanta," she said. "When I was there, I learned to speak with him all the time; to always know that he was with me, and I also learned to listen to and follow the sound current." She paused, searching the frightened face. Color was returning to his face, as though inwardly he was creeping back from the dead. "I have every confidence in your ability to succeed," Deetra said firmly.

Tolar's eyes met Deetra's. He smiled faintly and shrugged his shoulders, "I really have no choice," he said hesitating. "There is nothing else for me to do."

Deetra looked at him questioningly.

"There's no other reason for me to live except to awaken spiritually," he said. "To become Askan is the only goal for me."

Deetra touched his shoulder lightly. The warmth of the gesture brought tears to his eyes. He looked away embarrassed. "You'll do just fine," Deetra said.

He raised his eyes to hers once more. "I know I will," he said.

CHAPTER 3

To Deetra's delight the discussion group at the Village Square grew in size. Each day there seemed to be one or two new persons and, within a few weeks, all the available bench space was taken and many sat on the lawn within the circle.

The village physician was the most consistent attendee and he participated with great enthusiasm. He usually sat on the middle bench directly across from Deetra and sharply at noon, he took his seat, calling the gathering to attention as he did. His name was Sonar and he was a remarkable man. Not only did the other villagers respect him as a physician but he proved valuable in every way. And now Deetra was to find out just how valuable he was.

On this particular day, after the physician had called the meeting to order, Deetra asked him if he knew of the herbal medicine called torba which grew in the fields outside the village. Sonar said that he did but refused to administer the herb because of its narcotic effects. It neither dulled pain nor made a patient feel better so he concluded that its value, if any, was little.

"And what of the legends told of the plant?" Deetra asked him. As a child she had heard stories of those who had achieved out-of-the-body experiences through use of the plant, and she knew that there were some in the village who used the drug.

"Would you trade your knowledge of Soul for a dizzy head and a squeamish stomach?" Sonar asked. "Of course not," he said, answering for her, "and neither would the teller of those legends."

"But I have heard that the plant gives one special powers," a woman called out. "My son uses it to deepen his perceptions."

"And what does your son do for work?"

"He does not work," she said.

"He does nothing then?" Sonar asked.

"He perceives illusion," she said. "And I have seen his powers."

"But he uses none of his normal facilities to progress himself, therefore his survival is limited. He cannot live long in that state," Sonar said. "Work and change mirror each other's images."

"That is true," Deetra said, motioning to the physician to complete his thought.

"I am finished." he said.

"It's an interesting statement you made, doctor," Deetra said, "because the very thing we have been discussing is reflections. It is true that work and change mirror each other's images, and it is also true that everything we think, feel and do mirrors or reflects in the condition of our lives."

The physician turned from Deetra and looked at the woman who had been defending her son's use of the plant.

Watching, Deetra could see the inner communication between the physician and the woman, and she knew that the boy was one of his patients. The boy had become an invalid from use of the plant.

And they touched on a great number of other topics during the discussion meetings. One woman asked how one person seemed to be born with good fortune while another met with defeat at every turn.

Deetra had studied the woman thoughtfully before answering, understanding that the woman was referring to a condition which existed in her own family.

[27]

"Sometimes," Deetra began, "we end our lives with a great many debts left unpaid. These debts may be coin or they may be on other levels. When we offend another person, even though we feel justified in doing so, we incur a karmic debt to that person. That is why it is the wise man who turns his back on an argument. He knows that war, even on a one-to-one scale only complicates things, compounding the difficulty into a great one. If a person should steal or kill, there must be like compensation for the acts. Likewise, the good acts one performs also draw compensation. So it is that if one should die without receiving just compensation—whether good or bad—when we are reborn we carry the accounts with us. Thus, some will have an easy time early in life, reaping the fruits of the past, and others will have a difficult time, paying the debts of the past.

"Much of our past-life karma surfaces in the early part of our lives. If we deal with it, face it as one faces responsibilites, then it will pass quickly. It we deny it, refuse to accept the justice of it, using devious means to skirt the circumstances, then it may follow us our entire lifetime and even be carried into the next."

Deetra stopped speaking. A long, thoughtful silence levied throughout those gathered. She could see that understanding was flickering among them and that they were searching within.

Another woman, who was quite old, brought up the subject of death. You could see the pain of fear on her face when she asked, and it was evident that she feared it for herself.

"Death is consciousness stepping out of the body," Deetra said, explaining. "Soul is the thinker of thoughts; *it* is the perceiver of emotions, and *it* is also that being within which watches everything that goes on about us. Soul remains alive eternally. At death, which we Askan call *trans-*

[*28*]

lation, this Soul consciousness moves out of the body, shedding it as one would shed torn and useless clothing." Deetra hesitated, studying the woman's face for further questions.

"How can consciousness survive without the body?" the old woman asked.

"It cannot survive in the physical plane without a body," Deetra said. "That is why we have a body so that we may experience the physical world."

"But what is there without a body?" another person asked.

"In the planes of matter, feelings and thought, there is what we believe there is," Deetra said. "If we believe there is a fluffy winged angel to carry us off, then that's what there is. If we believe that we will burn in the fires of hell, then that is the experience waiting for us." She paused, aware of the confusion which was unsettling the participants. "The physical world is but a reflection of the invisible worlds. How we envision our life here is how we live it. That is why there is great benefit to live as an Askan or at least to reach for that attainment. The more aware we become, the more illusion is stripped away from us, the less limited we are as Soul. We can reach above the plane of angels into the pure positive God worlds and exist there unrestrained by emotions and physical-type images."

"I am an old woman," the elderly one said, trying to sit erect, "I cannot become Askan. There isn't time for me to reach Awakening Day."

"Although Awakening Day has its place in the physical realm, it is outside of time and space. If you reach for it, you will be working in the invisible realm, toward freedom from the physical."

The old woman rose from her seat. "And how do I begin?" she asked.

"Call upon the Hanta in your heart," Deetra said. "He will help you begin."

[*29*]

Although the classes provided a most joyful experience for Deetra, she could not help notice that in moments alone there grew another feeling. At first she could not describe it to herself and believed it to be a feeling of loneliness because it came after great outpouring of energy, when she had given her all in some way. But then, gradually, she realized it was something else.

It was not loneliness.

It was longing.

After class, she would often sit for long periods thinking nothing but listening to the up-turned volume of the sound current. The thin high-pitched sound of Soul seemed to dominate her physical environment and in listening to it, it transferred her into the depth of a void, connecting to her Soul. The void, the nothingness was really an allness, a oneness with her and she knew that if *it* had a name at all, *its* name was God the SUGMAD.

She was listening to the voice of God.

The longing was a longing for God, and the more she gave of herself, the more pronounced the longing became. It was bittersweet, both joyous and painful. It was what made her eager to respond to its urge and it was what reminded her that she was mortal. She knew she could not truly merge with *it* while in the physical body and yet the body provided her a means to be a co-worker with *it*.

She had sat up late one evening thinking on these things, listening to the voice of God, when she looked up suddenly to see the old messenger, standing in the open doorway to her room. Deetra was startled by his sudden appearance but not surprised. It had surprised her more that she had not seen him in some days, yet in looking up she wondered why he was there.

"May the blessings Be!" she said in greeting.

"Baraka Bashad!" the messenger said, returning the greeting.

Deetra had expected him to turn about and leave but

instead the old messenger moved into the room, drew up a chair and sat opposite her.

Deetra sat up straight, meeting his gaze. "May I be of assistance?" she asked.

"It is I who am to be of assistance to you," he said, smiling.

She had never seen the old messenger smile and it surprised her. "In what way?" she asked.

"In what way would you like assistance?" the old messenger asked.

"I can think of none," she said.

"Then I shall choose it," the old man said, raising the finger of his right hand in exclamation.

There was something in the gesture which seemed familiar to Deetra but she was unsure what and did not answer.

I see you do not know who I am," the old man said.

"You are the sanctuary messenger," Deetra said.

"Am I?"

Deetra studied the lines of the wrinkled old face. In them she saw the face of one she had seen many times about the sanctuary and many times in service to the Hanta. He was a figure who was well-known to all, especially to her. Had he not always seemed about her? In the very beginning he had handed her the crystal which led to her unfoldment as an Askan, and he had been seemingly close at hand ever since.

"You met me many times and yet one other time," the old man said, shifting his gaze to a faraway point behind her. He remained silent, as if deep in thought for what seemed a long while.

Then Deetra noticed another image overlapping his, one that was strangely familiar. She had seen it once and talked with it. It was after she had made her decision to marry Ian after his transfiguration to Hanta. It had been a difficult decision, not because she had been unsure of her love, but because of the magnitude of the responsibility he had accepted. She too would bear the burden of it. But there had been no choice for her heart. She loved Ian, and if he was to be Hanta, she was to be his wife regardless of the burden. It was then, at the moment of decision, that Malitara Tatz had suddenly appeared. He had promised to assist her when assistance was needed and had then disappeared.

Now Deetra saw that overlapping the image of the old messenger was the image of a young man, sturdy in frame, dark-skinned, bearded, and wearing a maroon tunic.

It was Malitara Tatz.

He had returned.

"You look surprised to see me," the man in the maroon tunic said. "You do remember me?"

Deetra nodded, too astonished to speak.

"As you can see," Malitara Tatz said, "I have rarely left your side. It's just that you never knew me in disguise." He motioned to himself, the two images of himself, one distinctly overlapping the other. For a moment he was two beings smiling, amused at Deetra's astonishment. Then quite suddenly, the image of the old messenger yielded, and disappeared. The man in the maroon tunic sat boldly before her.

"But who are you really?" Deetra asked shyly.

"I have already told you," Malitara Tatz said. "I once held the rod of power as Ian holds it now. I am your friend and as I once told you, it is my intention to serve you as guide on the journey to God-Realization."

Deetra recalled how when she had mentioned Malitara Tatz's name to Ian, he had responded warmly, stating that the man was their friend and to be trusted. Yet she wondered why the disguise; why Malitara Tatz could not have presented himself to her as himself in the beginning when he first handed her the crystal to prepare for Awakening Day. It seemed so long ago and so many episodes of which he had been a part.

"You were not ready," Malitara Tatz said, knowing her thought. "The time is now not before now."

"You have succeeded in understanding the laws of the lower worlds. The astral, causal and mental worlds no longer trouble you, although the latter is sometimes questionable," Malitara Tatz said, punctuating his statement by stabbing the air with his index finger. "It seems you enjoy the mental plane," he said again.

She smiled, remembering how the old messenger had often appeared, watching her from the doorway as she studied the ancient scrolls.

"But you have also given of your self and it seems that you've discovered the joy of giving," Malitara Tatz said.

"I know there is no greater privilege than serving as a channel for the Divine Force," Deetra said.

"Ah, that is it!" Malitara Tatz said. "And so you are ready to continue your education."

Deetra appeared puzzled.

Malitara Tatz laughed. "I do not mean to stick your nose in the scrolls studying," he said. "I mean it is time for you to prepare for the next step."

"Which is?" she asked.

"When you have discovered it , you will have taken it," Malitara Tatz said.

"And how will you help me?" Deetra said.

"I am an Askan master, which means I am a master of the detached state," Malitara Tatz said. "Surely if you open your heart and your ears you will learn something."

Deetra was embarrassed to have asked the question, yet her embarrassment appeared foolish and she quickly dismissed it. This being seemed so different than Ian who was also an Askan master, or from Ramus-i-Ramriz whom she had met on the causal plane. Malitara Tatz's manner was abrupt, direct and exceedingly firm and although his face was kind, it was plain that he meant to move her along the path as quickly as she allowed herself to go.

[*33*]

"What is it you wish me to do?" Deetra asked.

"You have opened the way to yourself," the Askan master said, "The way you have chosen will lead you. Meanwhile, there are certain things that you still do not have clearly at hand."

Deetra did not ask, but waited, studying the unusual lines of the master's face. His beard was trimmed short, close-cropped about his square jaw and his eyes, although calm, were exceedingly quick. He caught her every movement and indeed her every thought.

"Pay attention," Malitara Tatz instructed. "You are no longer a student learning to control mind. Do not let your thoughts amble about my face now. If you wish to do so there will be plenty of time to engage in such play in memory after I am gone."

Deetra drew herself erect, focusing her attention on the tisra til, that point between the eyes in the center of her forehead.

Malitara Tatz nodded appreciatively. "Now we will continue," he said. He drew in a deep breath. "You have been telling your class at the Village Square what it is like to be Askan," he said, pausing.

"Yes" she said.

"You must also explain to the people that Askan is only a word and that there are many words which mean Askan," he said, continuing. "The word Askan has power in this village only because it is the only word known to mean 'awakened one.' Because no one has understood this there is some superstition which has built up over the name itself. The superstition must stop. Do you understand me?"

Deetra nodded that she did.

"Good. Then let us continue on to the next point, which is that Awakening Day does not exist outside of the individual," Malitara Tatz said, pausing again.

Deetra did not try to hide her surprise.

"Somehow, many centuries ago, the idea got all mixed

up and it was believed that awakening could only come once in a hundred years. Did you not ever think this fact ridiculous?" he asked.

She did not answer but instead waited for the master to continue.

"The lazy ones started it," Malitara Tatz said. "They didn't want the responsibility of awakening so they set a date one hundred years ahead and talked about it to their children and their children to their children. Surely you have heard of the village promise?"

"Yes," Deetra said, "That once every hundred years the villages would prepare themselves for the event. Eventually through incarnation after incarnation everyone would succeed in the awakening promise."

"And it has been a slow, slow process," Malitara Tatz said. "There is no hurry for anyone to awaken, however there are many who are ready only they believe that they cannot until the hundred years is up. The myth must be destroyed. The lazy must be recognized for their laziness and those ready to continue to prepare themselves must be encouraged.

"And there is one other thing. It is the third and last item on your public notice," the master said, pausing.

"An individual's true identity," Deeta said, "which is Soul."

"Yes." The Askan master rose from his seat and stood broad-legged in front of her. "Soul has no age. It is formless and has no disposition. Yet even Askan initiates often neglect to notice that Soul resides positively in the negative force." He paused, allowing his words to sink deeply.

Deetra held her attention.

"If we do not allow ourselves to be swayed by the negative force," Malitara Tatz began, "if we do not respond to it when it presents itself to us, it negates itself and becomes positive. It thrives only in attachment, mainly self identification, which leads me to a point which you have

[*35*]

not fully grasped. Listen closely.

"When someone tells you of their experiences and you listen, you often identify yourself with what you hear. It is easy to identify with others' feelings because we have them ourselves, perhaps the same feelings only about different things. You and I both feel hungry after a long walk, yet our tastes may vary. You understand?"

Deetra nodded.

"Then let me tell you this," the master said, striking the air with his index finger as he spoke. "Identification with another's feelings is a trap. You must not acknowledge the same feelings within yourself in thought as another speaks. If you do, you attach yourself to that feeling and take on the other person's karma, which is foolish indeed. Am I making myself clear?"

Deetra looked up at him, uncertain.

Malitara Tatz sat down again opposite her. "Since we all have feelings," he said, "we cannot help recognizing the feelings of others. But as soon as we say to ourselves that we understand another's feelings, when the teller is expressing them, we are becoming attached to what we are hearing. Next thing you know we must live out an episode of the same feeling in order to complete the cycle of karma and rid ourselves of it."

"But how can you listen to a person sharing a feeling and not mentally comment on it?" Deetra asked.

"Ah, now you have it!" Malitara Tatz said. "You recognize through Soul, that is Soul knows but mind does not think about the knowing. As long as mind does not think on it, there is no attachment and no karmic tie."

Deetra was struck by the idea.

"I can see that you understand," the Askan master said. "This is perhaps one of the most important things you will ever learn. I say this because knowledge of this fact is a liberator. It is a key to the detached state."

Deetra's attention broke and she drifted distantly in

thought. What the Askan adept had said made a grave impression on her and for the first time she understood how she could be free from mind, as well as influence from the will of others. It was the answer to a question she once craved to know and had given up trying to comprehend. Now it was given to her.

Malitara Tatz touched her lightly on the arm, patting her and she smiled appreciatively. "It took me many years to fully grasp that knowledge," he said softly. "It seems it must be earned and, until it is, the explanation means little, mere words for the mind to grasp. A great spiritual adept once said 'True spirtuality cannot be taught; it must be caught'. I think you understand now what that statement means."

"Yes," she said, filled with the sudden warmth of the master's presence. She no longer felt uncomfortable in his presence and she understood why he had chosen to assist her on the path to God-Realization, and she knew that the warmth she felt from this man came from her as well. It was gratitude. "Thank you," she said.

"We will leave off here for tonight," Malitara Tatz said. "We will continue another time, when you are ready."

Deetra studied the firm set of the bearded man's face. She understood what the master meant. She needed time now to experience the freedom of this detachment that had opened up for her.

"In the service which awaits you," the adept said, "remember that you have the right to reject as well as accept. It is not necessary for you to take on everything which comes your way. View your choices from the causal plane and use discrimination." He hesitated, looking deeply into her. "Do not look so relieved," he said, laughing lightly, "I will not be leaving you for long."

Then he turned and walked toward the door to her chamber. As he reached it, he said "Baraka Bashad!" It was the old messenger's voice and the man who walked through the doorway was the old messenger.

[*37*]

CHAPTER 4

Deetra had not seen the student Tolar for some time and so she was both delighted and surprised when he presented himself at the conclusion of her noonday class. She was sitting on a bench rerolling some parchments when suddenly she looked up and saw him there. His face was drawn and sober and the skin around his eyes was dark as though he had been sick.

"Tolar!" Deetra said brightly, "how nice to see you. It has been some time."

"Yes," he answered, nodding. "I wondered if the Hanta had returned."

Deetra studied the seriousness on the man's face. He obviously felt himself in grave danger of something. "He has not returned as yet," she said, "but he is expected at the new moon."

"Can you tell me where to find him?" Tolar asked.

"There is some urgency to this matter?" Deetra asked, acknowledging the gravity in his tone of voice.

"Yes, I must see him at once."

It was easy for Deetra to look into the man's mind. He was so disturbed that the disturbance showed on his face and spoke loudly through his eyes. Even so she did not need to look into Tolar's eyes to know his thoughts. There was an aura of fear about him which told the story in distorted images. Though he said nothing, Deetra knew that he was under attack by the negative forces within his own being. He was meeting himself in combat—the positive and the

[*38*]

negative sides of himself at war with each other—but was unaware that the battle cries came from within. She knew clearly that he was projecting his difficulties into the environment as she had once done in becoming an Askan.

"The Hanta is in grave danger," Tolar said. "It's not anything I have been told but something that I see myself. There is turmoil building within the village."

"In what way?"

"It's difficult to pinpoint but I can feel it there," Tolar said. "The Hanta has been gone too long and his presence is sorely missed."

"Well I can surely agree that he is missed," Deetra said lightly.

Tolar smiled faintly. "I'm sorry I couldn't come to our spiritual law class," he said, "but I have been so very busy with the affairs of Moonwalk."

"We have missed you," Deetra said, aware that the man was in desperate mental straits. The crossing of Moonwalk was not an easy task and she felt compassion for the man's struggle, remembering how he so very much wanted the experiences of Soul awakening, recalling the joy on his face when the old messenger handed him a crystal as a tool to begin. At the memory, she glanced up to see if the old messenger was about now but saw that he was not. "Do you have your crystal?" she asked Tolar.

He nodded and looked away.

"Do you carry it with you?" Deetra asked again.

Tolar shook his head slowly, not looking at Deetra.

She waited, studying the intensity pouring through the man's face.

Hesitantly, he turned to face her. "I lost it," he said, his voice trembling. His eyes filled with tears, showing that he had suffered greatly from the experience.

"How was that?" Deetra asked, prodding.

"I was at home. I had taken the crystal from my pocket and placed it on the table. There was a knock at the door which I answered. It was the same old woman who had visited me many times before, only this time her manner changed. She voiced no obscenities and she brought no gifts." Tolar hesitated, wringing his hands in the silence. "She merely asked for water and her manner was so pathetic that I could not refuse her. I asked her to wait but while I went for the water, she entered the room and stole my crystal. When I returned she had gone. The crystal had gone." He looked away quickly. A sob escaped his throat. "I don't know what to do," he said. "I must see the Hanta. The woman may try to offend him."

"There is little danger of that," Deetra said gently.

"But she is turning the villagers against him," Tolar said, catching control of his emotions. "I can see it in the people's faces and in their actions."

Deetra did not respond but looked sorrowfully at the older man. She wanted to help but knew there was nothing for her to do. She could not interfere with an experience Tolar had chosen for himself. It was something he had to work through by himself. Nor could she offer advice on the matter unless asked. It was the Askan way, not to interfere with another's state of consciousness. How could she tell Tolar that the Hanta was invincible; that to go out and seek him was unnecessary because he was always near even though he may be physically travelling elsewhere; that the danger Tolar sensed for Hanta was really that which he feared for himself. He did not yet realize that the crystal was merely symbolic, a gift from the master which meant that the student was ready to begin. Once received it could never be stolen by another. It could only be purposely discarded by its owner.

Seeing Tolar in this state stirred her memory of a few years back when she had journeyed through Moonwalk and what she had experienced. She had been frightened many times on that journey. It had seemed that it would never end—adventure upon adventure merely for the purpose of pointing out the illusions of life and how she controlled her own experiences, chose them via her state of consciousness. She had felt alone too, but not completely. She had always felt the Hanta to be with her even if she could not always see him. There seemed always to be an invisible protection around her.

"Do you not call on the Hanta for assistance?" Deetra asked.

"He is not here," Tolar said, visibly upset. "If he were here I would ask."

"But surely you have become aware of the inbetween planes of existence," Deetra said.

Tolar stared at her for a long while before answering. He knew that she referred to Moonwalk. She had mentioned it to him before, the last time they had talked. The name was not new to him. All the villagers repeated tales of the terrible Moonwalk where one had to trod in order to become Askan. It was said that hideous beings attacked the adventurer and that all sorts of adversity awaited in hidden traps. But every person had a different tale of what Moonwalk was and he knew that they were all legend. Yet he knew the meaning of Moonwalk was something of importance or else Deetra would not have mentioned it to him.

"It is real," Deetra said. "Moonwalk exists, just as you and I exist."

"You mean the village stories are true," Tolar said.

"They are true for the one telling them," Deetra said. "But only you can describe your own Moonwalk. It is a place within the individual. It is the hidden part of one's self, filled with evil and confusion and symbols which we have accepted and which have aberrated our lives." She paused, studying the confusion on Tolar's face. "The villagers tell tales of Moonwalk because they are not aware of what they are telling. To them it is only a scary place and it is exciting and fun to tell. But you never hear an Askan tell tales of Moonwalk and yet they have all been consciously there."

"But why?" Tolar asked.

"Because for each of us Moonwalk is different. My experiences are not the same as anyone else's, and neither are yours. There are some similarities, such as the result of our experiences and many of the symbols we encounter along the way. But our adventures are individual and so is our perception of them."

"What of the symbols?" Tolar asked.

"You will come to understand that yourself in time," Deetra answered. "There is little I can tell you of them, except a clue that symbols are not always as we expect them. I used to believe them to be outside of myself and then I realized that they were actually coming from within, that is I saw that everything significant in my world was a symbol of my perception of it." She paused, drawing in a deep breath. "You said, Tolar, that you were busy with the affairs of Moonwalk. What did you mean?"

Tolar hesitated, unsure.

"Could it be that you do not accept the presence of the inbetween worlds?" Deetra asked. "That you believe that everything is without and that nothing is within?"

"I know that the 'within' exists," Tolar said quickly. "It's just that I don't understand it."

"Do you wish to tell me what you don't understand?" Deetra asked.

"I don't know what to say, but yes, I do want to tell you," Tolar said.

Deetra waited silently.

"All this talk about inbetween worlds, it just doesn't make any sense to me," Tolar said. "The inbetween worlds are inbetween what?"

"Between the veil of the seen and the unseen," Deetra said, softly.

"But how can I know the unseen?"

"Through your inner senses," Deetra said.

[*42*]

"And how is that?"

"Imagination is our inner sight," Deetra said.

"But imagination is illusion. It is untruth," Tolar said.

Deetra studied the confusion on the man's face and she understood why he had been suffering. "Do you not remember our many discussions on imagination in our spiritual law class?" Deetra asked.

Tolar shook his head. "I wish I did," he said. "I have got to have some answers."

"Imagination is the gateway to reality. It projects our state of consciousness from the unseen to the seen," Deetra said. "It is the one faculty in mankind that sets us apart from animals. It empowers Soul to recognize itself. The unseen when viewed through imagination becomes seen and we can then understand at last what it is that manifests in our physical world. But first we must recognize it. Finally when one reaches a consciousness of Soul, the visible is no longer a reality and the invisible world no longer a dream or a fantasy." She paused, looking deeply into the student's eyes. "I can see a flicker of understanding," she said lightly. "A more enriched realization of what I am saying will come in time."

"But I cannot wait!" Tolar said.

Deetra smiled. "I too have been impatient," she said, "but pushing against the door of Soul only makes it more difficult to open. Relax and live your experiences with the joy of learning." She paused again. There was a sudden panic on Tolar's face. "You are not alone," she said again. "You think the Hanta must return to the village to help you but you need only call upon his assistance, visualizing him in your imagination and he will come to you and assist in every way."

Tolar did not answer but stood motionless staring at the brilliant blue of his teacher's eyes. He had always thought Deetra to be a strange being and though he still believed this to be true, he saw now that he was transforming into a similar being himself. Perhaps that was why he was struggling so. If he accepted the power of imagination who knows what awaited him. Oftentimes he felt as one who is losing his mind. If mind should lose control of his world what would become of him? Then he recalled a passage of the scripture he had first been given to study when embarking on the path of the Askan. It read that mind was a machine and as such was a useful tool but a poor master. The master, the inner master called Soul, would one day awaken and take control. Yet mind, the scripture had said, would not yield without struggle and yet it was the struggle which prompted it to yield.

Tolar smiled weakly at Deetra. "You mean the Hanta will be here now if I ask it of him?" he asked.

Deetra nodded. "But you must ask," she said.

"Then I do ask," Tolar said. "I ask the Hanta to be here now."

"Then he is," Deetra said reasurringly. "He is here. I can surely feel his presence."

Tolar studied the sincerity on Deetra's face. There was no doubt that she believed the Hanta to be with her. If only he could be sure.

"You may find it helpful to put your questions aside," Deetra said, "and practice the presence of the master. Talk to him in your thoughts and visualize him on the screen of your mind. Proof will follow." She glanced away to the shift of the afternoon sun. It was growing late in the day. "I must go now," she said, turning back to Tolar. "There is still much I must accomplish this day. I am sure you will find the way to communicate with the Hanta."

Tolar nodded. "I'm sure I will," he said, "since I must. And thank you for being a friend."

Deetra heard no more from Tolar until one afternoon following the village discussion class, the physician Sonar waited to speak with her. He waited until the others had dispersed and were leaving the square and then he approached her.

"Tolar has been quite sick," the physician said, "and there is little I can do for him. It may be helpful if you will pay him a visit."

"What is wrong?" Deetra asked, looking up from her seat on the bench. The physician's expression showed some concern.

"It happened quite suddenly," Sonar said, "or at least it seemed that way. I saw him in the morning of one day and that same afternoon he came to me with a burning fever. I have not been able to break it."

"When was this?" Deetra asked.

"He came to me the day before yesterday," Sonar said.

Deetra hesitated, listening for the shrill pitched voice of SUGMAD. As her inner sense perceived it, she rose from her seat. "Of course I will go with you," she said to the physician.

The student Tolar was lying in deep sleep on a mat inside the physician's chamber. He looked as though he could have been dead and the physician went immediately to him to verify he wasn't. After examining Tolar, he rose up and turned to Deetra. "He is in a coma, meaning he is both asleep and awake. I believe him to be conscious of us, but who knows."

Deetra nodded that she understood, appreciative of the physician's perceptiveness, and knelt down next to Tolar. "May we be alone?" she asked.

The physician looked at her questioningly.

"I will call if there is any change," Deetra said.

Sonar stood hesitantly, stretching his lower lip between his thumb and forefinger as though considering her request, then he turned abruptly and left the chamber.

Deetra turned to Tolar, tilting the man's head to face her. His eyes were open wide and staring but seeing nothing. Her gaze gently swept about his face, resting lightly on his tisra til, the spiritual eye located above the eyebrows and to the center of his forehead. Moments passed but gradually she began to penetrate the inner sanctum of her student. She knew she was violating the most private sanctum of the individual, but she also knew that since he was her student she did have the right, although her responsibility would still be great. Gently, while looking at him in this way, she began to chant the ancient sound of SUG-MAD, the HU-HUuuuuu, HUuuuuuu, HUuuuuuu.

And then she saw.

Tolar was standing alone in the inbetween worlds in a place where no scenery existed. His body was wrapped in a thin pink fiber which spiralled about him from his feet to his head. His eyes were open and as Deetra saw him, he saw her too.

"Help me!" he called in distant whisper. "Help me!"

Her heart swelled with compassion for the man. It was not the first time she had seen someone trapped by the negative force. The pink fiber about him symbolized that his own emotions held him prisoner. "You must help yourself," Deetra said firmly.

"But I cannot. I have no strength left," Tolar said weakly.

"Do you want to die?" Deetra asked. "Do you want to die in this state where you will have to begin again?"

"No ... please help me," Tolar pleaded. His breath choked. He was sobbing. "Please help me."

"Call on the Hanta!" Deetra instructed.

"He is not here. You are here."

Deetra studied the condition of the man. He was so out of control that if she did help him, she would have to carry his burden and she knew that she could not do it. He would have to help himself by calling on the Hanta. "The

Hanta is here if you want him," Deetra said firmly. "But you must call him yourself."

"You call him for me," Tolar said sobbing.

"That would do no good," Deetra said, trying to prod him. "The Hanta is here with me already."

"Then ask him to help me," Tolar said, pleading.

"You must ask him yourself."

"I cannot."

"But you must."

There was a long, deathly silence in which Deetra asked the Hanta to guide her. The Holy One's radiant form seemed to consume her, to move in and through her and where she began and *it* ended she was uncertain. In that moment of yielding to *it* she had placed the fate of the student Tolar in the Hanta's arms. And in that moment, she heard the student Tolar call out to the Hanta for help.

The pink fibers which had been wrapped about Tolar were no longer there. In the recluse of his mind she saw he was free and running wildly across a long stretch of sun-bleached terrain. As he ran he called to the Hanta for help and as he did so, gradually the terrain changed from barren to light, leafy vegetation. It was a good sign. Although he was still being controlled by his own emotion he was reaching out of himself and in reaching out, he would gradually find release.

Tolar's outward appearance changed as well. He was beginning to perspire profusely, thrashing uncomfortably on his sleeping mat.

Deetra called to the physician to re-enter the chamber.

Sonar appeared in the doorway and quickly came to Tolar's side. "The fever has broken," he said with some relief. "Somehow I knew you could do it."

"I did not do it," Deetra said firmly.

Sonar turned to face her. "Then you were the channel for it to happen," he said. "Whatever, I am grateful, and I'm sure Tolar will be too. If only I had stuck with the Force when it was given to me." The physician hesitated and turned to Deetra. "If only I had stuck with it," he said again. "I could be such a great healer as a channel."

Deetra questioned the deep-set lines of the physician's face.

"You probably have guessed it by now," Sonar said.

"Guessed what?"

"I have become an avid student of yours," he said.

"Yes you have, and you are also quite aware for one just beginning," Deetra said.

"Well then you know," Sonar said seriously.

"Know?"

Sonar glanced back at Tolar and patted the semi-conscious man on the arm, then turned back to Deetra. "Let me show you something," Sonar said, rising.

The physician went to a box on a ledge over the fireplace and returned to where Deetra was sitting. Then he opened it.

The object lit up.

It was a crystal.

Deetra looked at the physician in surprise.

"You did not know then?"

"No."

"I thought the Askan knew everything," Sonar said.

"As it is necessary and purposeful," Deetra said.

"You really did not know?" Sonar asked again.

"No. Would you like to tell me about it?" she asked.

Sonar lifted the crystal from the box and held it cupped in the palm of his hand. "I've had it a long time," he said. "It was given to me when I was a boy, a young boy. As you can see that was a long time ago." He hesitated, smiling. A streak of sunlight entered the room and rested on him, exaggerating the white of his hair.

"When I was a boy," he said, "the sanctuary messenger gave me this crystal, telling me that it was 'Hanta's gift to me.' Then he said, 'What you do with it will be your gift to Hanta.'" The physician paused thoughtfully. "I regret," he said, "that until now I did nothing with it."

"You mean you put it away just after you received it?" Deetra asked, seeing an image of the old messenger giving him the crystal, and glancing about the room half expecting to see him near. She had not seen him since that night in her chamber.

Sonar lowered his head and slowly raised it again. "Yes," he said, nodding. "I put it away and told no one about it."

"But why?" Deetra asked. "You were ready or else you would not have received it."

"Yes, I was ready but I did not want to be," the physician said thoughtfully. "I was a good looking young man with a thousand dreams to fulfill. I could not turn my back on them at the time."

"And now?" Deetra asked. "Can you turn your back on them now?"

"It's a peculiar thing," Sonar said, "all of the dreams I had were fulfilled, save one."

"Which is?"

"To heal with the divine power," the physician said. "Do you think me foolish?"

"Not at all."

"It is possible then?"

"It is not for me to say."

"But is it?"

"It is possible."

"Will you help me?" Sonar asked, extending his hand.

Deetra stared at the outstretched hand, marveling at the unusual twist in affairs since she had started teaching the villagers. "I will do what I can," she said, "but mostly you must help yourself."

"I'll find the old messenger and tell him," the physician said, rising to his feet anxiously.

"That is not necessary," Deetra said. "What is important now is that you begin to work with the crystal. Carry it with you and work with it. Get to know its usefulness as a tool, and most important of all, ask the Hanta's assistance."

"I will," Sonar said, closing his fingers about the crystal. "I will as soon as he returns."

Deetra let out a sigh. "It is not necessary to wait until he returns," she said, feeling as though she had repeated herself many times already. "The Hanta is with you always if you ask him to be. Talk to him in your thoughts. Picture his image in your mind while focusing your attention on the tisra til, the spiritual eye in the center of your forehead." She paused, tapping the spot just above her eyebrows with her index finger. "The rest will all come about naturally."

"But what of Tolar?" the physician asked, motioning to the man lying on the floor beneath them.

"He did not seek the Hanta in his heart, nor did he practice the presence of the Hanta in his life. He tried to do it all alone. Without the Hanta, you cannot make the journey through Moonwalk." Deetra stopped, allowing her words to penetrate. She could see that the physician was greatly disturbed by them.

"I cannot lean upon another man," Sonar said.

"He is not just another man," Deetra said. "He is the master."

"Nor can I accept a master!" Sonar said. "If one is a master then the other is a slave, or at best a servant."

Was this also Tolar's problem?

Was it more difficult for a man to accept another man as his master than it was for a woman?

Deetra had had no such difficulty.

Suddenly she remembered Malitara Tatz's warning— that she was not to try to identify with another's experiences; that to do so formed a mental trap. She quickly collected herself. "I think you misunderstand the meaning of the Hanta," Deetra said firmly. "The Hanta is not the master of people but of the detached state of consciousness. In our relationship with him, he acts as a guide through the lower worlds such as Moonwalk. He assists us by teaching us what we need to know in the inner planes. He is a friend, not someone to be feared. He is the carrier of Divine Love which he bestows upon us freely without expectation. He will only assist if asked and only then does this assistance come to us in the inner planes. Tolar is now, at last, learning to ask for help." She paused, studying the uncertainty on the physician's face. "Do you understand me?" she asked.

Sonar opened his clenched fist and stared at the crystal. The sunlight darted through it, reflecting a myriad of color in the room. He drew in a deep breath and closed his hand about it again, clutching it closely to his breast. "I think I do," he said huskily. "I hope I do."

His sincerity deeply touched Deetra and she relaxed. Smiling, she gently touched the hand holding the crystal. "May the blessings Be!" she said. "May the blessings Be!"

CHAPTER 5

It seemed the physician was not the only one among the villagers to have been given a crystal at an early age only to tuck it away to discover it again at a later point in life. There were a number of others, who Deetra came to learn about through the course of talking to each individually, and knowledge of this fact greatly increased her sense of responsibility. She was sitting alone one evening in her chamber thinking on it when suddenly she had the idea that the village class had an established identity. The idea struck her strangely at first but gradually she came to see that there was a bond between each of them, especially the crystal bearers, just as there had been a bond between her, Rian and Curtser on their joint journey through Moonwalk long ago.

As she thought about it, she focused her attention on the individuals involved, seeing them, watching them, from the point of Soul, as if she were witnessing actors in a play. The setting was Moonwalk. It was an individual Moonwalk for each of them and yet, since they maintained a group entity, the overall image of it was the same for all. The overall image was the scenery.

The scenery was similar to that of the village, a somewhat mountainous terrain which, although barren in spots, was also lush with greenery. The sight was quite beautiful and in it were small, tame animals and a few large ones. There was harmony and love among the partcipants and, as a result, there was balance. The Hanta was in the heart of each and therefore his radiant form reflected in the peace and serenity of the environment. However, occasionally, an imbalance took place in the individual lives of the participants and a wave of psychic energy fluttered thoughout the scenery. It was in these times that the individuals gathered together and chanted the HU until the balance had been regained. They were strong students of the Force and their strength seemed to come from their togetherness. Could it be that their karmic ties had been formed some eons ago; that they had held their crystals in waiting all these years until they could come together as a unit again to share the unit's strength?

Deetra was fascinated by the idea.

Was it so?

And if it were true, was it not also true that her role as class teacher made her a part of that entity?

"And now you are prepared for the next step," a voice said from across the room.

Deetra looked up to see Malitara Tatz coming toward her. He sat opposite her, his white teeth bared in a wide smile.

"And now let us continue, " the maroon robed figure said, sitting before her.

Deetra sat up straight in her chair, thinking she had not seen the old messenger for quite some time, but then Malitara Tatz was the old messenger.

"And was there a purpose for you to see him?" the Askan adept asked, hearing her thought.

"No," Deetra said, "It's just that I had grown so accustomed to seeing him."

"Neither of us have been very far away," Malitara Tatz said, smiling broadly.

Deetra returned his smile, aware of the adept's presence. His physical presence charged the atmosphere in her chamber. She was glad to see him and anxious to share the experiences with the villagers.

"Do you know what it is that you have just touched upon?" Malitara Tatz asked.

"The group entity of the class," Deetra said.

"Yes, but there is more," the master said.

Deetra was unsure and did not answer.

"You noticed that the appearance of Moonwalk was the same for everyone within the group entity; that is the scenery of it," Malitara Tatz said. "Even though each individual has individual experiences, their experiences all take place in a location they all see the same way." He paused, studying the expression on Deetra's face." Let me put it another way," the adept said, striking the air with his index finger in his accustomed manner. "When individuals merge together in an area of space for the purpose of spiritual understanding, they are aware of the bond linking them. If, however, they are not gathered for the purpose of spiritual understanding, the result is the same only lacking awareness of the bond."

Deetra could not hide her confusion.

Malitara Tatz laughed, slapping his hand on his leg. "I will put it very plainly," he said comically, "if you are ready."

Deetra nodded attentively.

"The people of this village have all chosen to live in this village. Even though some stay because they were born here, or their families remain here, or they wouldn't know where else to go, they are still here by choice; that is, no one is holding them. If they truly wished to leave, they could simply walk out. Do you understand?"

"Yes," Deetra said.

"Good. Now the next point is that all the people living here have agreed upon the image of what their village is like; that is, the basic visuals are the same. Do you understand?"

"Yes," Deetra said. "You mean they have an agreed upon image of what the village looks like."

[*54*]

"Exactly," Malitara Tatz said, "Exactly. But let us make it clear that the agreed upon image in no way interferes with the individual's perceptions of what he experiences. It simply says our village is in a valley, surrounded by jagged mountains and flanked to the East by a dense forest. The village homes are round cottages intersected by dirt paths all meeting at the Village Square. You follow me?"

"I think so," Deetra said.

"Good, then you are ready to see that the appearance of a village, as well as its natural scenery, is determined by the people who live in it. It is the result of the group entity."

"But the natural scenery as well?" Deetra asked distantly, suddenly aware that she had answered her own question by understanding the element of choice made by each individual in the location of their village.

"Good, now you've got it!" Malitara Tatz said. "Now listen closely. Up until this point we have been speaking of the exterior village but there is also an interior one." He paused to catch her expression. "Actually, the interior came first."

"As above, so below," Deetra said, quoting from the scriptures.

"Precisely!" the adept said. "And so when people are seen gathered together in the physical environment, they are also gathered together in the invisible environment, the latter existing first. And so those who have the bond between them experience the appearance of the invisible worlds in the same way. That is why you are able to reach so many varied individuals in one class. The common meeting ground on the inner exists."

Deetra did not speak but sat silently thinking on what the adept had said, marvelling at the clarity existing in the scheme of life. It was so clear, so precise, so interwoven with the beings residing in the physical world and invisible worlds, that no mere human being could conceive of such a plan. It was wonderful, enacted by the God-Force, dreamed into being by the Supreme Deity, the Formless One, the SUGMAD. It was greater than miracles. It was perfect.

Malitara Tatz was looking at her, smiling gently. "And now you see and understand," he said.

Deetra's eyes met his. She had a sudden feeling that she was no longer attached to her body, but floating somewhere outside it. In the spiritual adept's eyes she saw a tiny image of herself and it was as though she was him seeing her, as if her consciousness transferred into him and while she was looking at him, she was also looking at herself.

How was it possible?

She was both herself and Malitara Tatz.

They were one and the same.

Or were they?

Just as quickly as the feeling had come upon her, it left. Malitara Tatz rose from his seat and, without word or motion, left her sitting there alone.

Deetra did not know how long she sat there. Her thoughts had been stilled by the sight of seeing from within the spiritual adept and in the silence she was able to continue seeing that way. She was herself but she was also Malitara Tatz and of which she was more seemed uncertain. Her vision of life was now twofold, viewing the inner and outer images simultaneously. Suddenly there was no separation between the two and as she perceived on one plane of existence she also perceived on the other. And it was an awareness without thought. It was a seeing, a knowing but moreover a perceiving and in it she was one with not only Malitara Tatz, but with all beings and all things and all beings and things were her.

The interaction, the yielding of herself, merging into the All, granted her the perception of all. There was nothing she did not know, nor no one she could not see. As her mind triggered images, she was that, and she could truly perceive the mechanics of the mind-machine and how it continually flashed images of things, as well as images of those who came within her realm of daily experience. She saw Tolar, Sonar the physician, and each member of her class, and also those she had not recently seen, such as Rian the scribe, Curtser the adventurer, Sarpent the Chief Elder and her husband Ian, the Hanta. She was them all and with each she lingered momentarily to capture the feeling of the beingness of each. Only when she came to the image of Ian, she went no further.

Perceiving her husband in this way was the true marriage, the height of a glorious union. They were truly one, without separation of any kind. They were the two halves made whole; the positive and the negative forces united; the plus and the minus merged into being a third entity, one of combined units. Together they were the everything and the *All* of everyone undivided without aspects of any kind. It was a union, a beingness, which was the *ALL,* the void, the nothingness of the great Divine Entity Itself. It was God, the SUGMAD.

There was light.

There was sound.

There was nothing else—no time, no space, no motion.

The thin, high-pitched scream of SUGMAD was the *All* of *All* and it tore into her without mercy, releasing her from all feeling of bodily life. There was only the Beingness now and the Beingness was both love and power and it stripped her of personality. She became *IT,* the love, the power, the source of *All* and *IT* was her, only her identity was no longer outside *IT.*

Then she stopped.

Deetra was herself again, not her same self, but the *IT* of SUGMAD, the Force of SUGMAD in her form.

Malitara Tatz stood next to her, his hand lightly resting

on her shoulder. She looked up at him and saw him smile.

"You have realized the God-Self."

Deetra did not answer, nor did she try to speak. She knew that the experience had changed her, yet she also knew that she was still herself. And she understood why she had a physical vehicle, a body in which to house the great power and love of the Formless One in her work as a channel in the lower worlds. A thrill ran through her and shook her body. She had been with the SUGMAD.

"Where does one go from here?" she asked humbly, tilting her head upward to where the spiritual adept stood.

"Everywhere and anywhere," Malitara Tatz said, smiling. "Your experience today is yet another beginning."

CHAPTER 6

Deetra was preparing to leave for her noonday class with the villagers when the old messenger suddenly entered her chamber.

Deetra smiled in greeting.

"There is great urgency," the old messenger said, leaning heavily upon his walking stick which he held in front of him. "There is no time for the village class. You must be on your way."

The smile disappeared from Deetra's face. "On my way to where?" she asked, studying the deep crevices on the old man's face. She knew the messenger to be the guise of Malitara Tatz, yet the spiritual adept did not disclose himself. His thoughts were as still as the air in her room.

"To the land of Nome," the old messenger said, his eyes firmly holding hers.

For an instant Deetra saw herself in his eyes and the feeling reminded her of the feeling she had experienced while looking into the eyes of Malitara Tatz; how she had felt one with him; had indeed become him, the adept, and how with her inner eyes she had become each person she imaged as well as all things she imaged. The feeling had lingered for what seemed a long while and there was a bittersweet quality to it. The inner seeing was bliss and yet the bliss was overpowering and seemingly painful. It was the same now. The memory was a moment etched in consciousness. It would always be with her she knew, coming to her, rising in her as something stirred it and that something could be anything or anyone.

"Be ready now," the old messenger said, tapping his stick upon the stone floor.

Deetra thought about the old messenger's presence. He asked that she be ready to leave for Nome but Nome, she knew, did not exist. It was a place mentioned in the scriptures as a meeting ground of consciousness. From what she had read of it she had not believed it to be within the worlds of form. "I do not understand," she said thoughtfully.

"Understanding comes with experience," the old messenger said. "You do not as yet have that experience, but you will if you hurry." He tapped his stick anxiously on the hard floor.

"But where do I go?" she asked.

"It is almost the new moon," the old man said.

"Yes, and then my husband Ian will return."

"There is no returning without passage through Nome," the old messenger said. "It is I who am to lead you, and it is time that we go." He turned abruptly and walked across the room and out her chamber door.

Deetra hurried after him.

The courtyard was nearly still. A single servant hurried from one end to the other, glancing her way and then disappearing through an archway which led to the kitchen. The thoughts of the one who passed were filled with preparations for the returning of the Hanta and those who had travelled with him, and Deetra knew that soon the courtyard, with its many intersections to various parts of the sanctuary, would be a busy place indeed. Deetra caught the thrill of it as she hurried past, following the way the old messenger had gone, and the thrill rippled through her.

She stepped into the open air outside the sanctuary and stopped. The old messenger had disappeared. Looking about, her eyes scanned the terrain, but he was not to be seen.

Where had he gone?

She listened inwardly for an answer. In the silence within there was a tiny whisper and it urged her to find the land of Nome.

But how?

It was not a place of form. She could not just go there in her physical body, and she knew that finding Nome was not purely an inner experience. The old messenger had clearly indicated that by insisting that she follow him outside the sanctuary walls.

She stood looking across the terrain.

Gradually she saw that someone was coming toward her. As he neared, he called out, waving his arms in gaining her attention. As the figure neared, she saw it was Sonar, the physician. She went toward him.

"You must come quickly," Sonar said, breathing heavily from his run across the field. "Old Estella is dying," he said, "and she is so terrified of it. She said that she fears herself not strong enough to cross over without yielding to the negative force."

Deetra studied the physician without answering.

"She needs you," the physician went on, "she refuses to let go until you are with her and the pain she is experiencing is overwhelming."

"Is it not your task to relieve that pain?" Deetra asked, uneasily.

"There is nothing I can do without contributing to a loss of consciousness and she does not wish to die in that way," he said.

Still Deetra hesitated. She thought of the old woman, remembering how in the village class she had expressed her fears of death, and how they had discussed the subject at length. It had seemed then that Estella had contented heself with the explanations.

"She has a crystal," the physician said anxiously.

Deetra looked deeply into the physician. He was greatly unnerved by the fact that she still hesitated in returning to Estella with him, yet in that moment the feeling slipped and became another. He was seeing Estella not as an old woman dying but as an entity reaching out for help in translating to another form or form of existence. He was seeing her as Soul.

A strange sensation prickled Deetra's flesh. Looking into the physician this way, she was not looking into his thoughts in the same way she had grown accustomed to knowing another's thoughts. Something was different. She was not merely listening to his inner voice, she was within him. His feelings were her feelings. In a sense she was feeling what he was feeling and knowing what he was knowing, thinking his thoughts, yet all the while she was detached and herself. She had become Sonar the physician just as she had become Malitara Tatz the evening before. Something in her had changed. Malitara Tatz had told her she had realized the God-Self. Today the old messenger came to lead her into the land of Nome. Was the physician to point the way?

"Will you come?" Sonar asked, pleading.

"Yes," Deetra said, motioning him to lead her. "Let us hurry."

The old woman rose up from her sleeping mat when Deetra entered the room, extending her hand to her. She appeared ancient with years. Deetra went to her, taking the warm, wrinkled old hand in hers and sat next to her on the floor so that the woman would lie down again.

"Sonar tells me you have a crystal," Deetra said softly.

"One which was never used," the old woman said. She spoke slowly as if the words were formed by great effort.

"Where is it?" Deetra asked.

The old woman opened her other hand, outstretched alongside the length of her bony body. The crystal lit up.

Deetra smiled. "The Hanta is with you," she said

lightly. "There is no doubt that your crystal is not idle now."

Estella raised her other arm and looked at the crystal. The light from a nearby window hit it and an array of color danced about the room. The old woman smiled, looking first at it and then at Deetra. "Thank you," she said.

"I have done nothing," Deetra said. "You have had the crystal all the while. You needed only to learn its secrets."

"It is too late for me," Estella said. "I have had it for over eighty years and did not learn its secrets. It is too late now."

"It is never too late," Deetra said gently.

"But I have no more time."

"To learn the secrets of the crystal does not require time," Deetra said, "it requires a certain consciousness."

The old woman searched Deetra's face for an answer.

"It requires a certain childlike attitude, both yielding and curious, as well as a willingness to accept the consequences." Deetra paused, waiting for reaction.

"It is too late," the old woman said. "I cannot yield that part of myself now which I have never been able to yield. The child in me ceased to exist at the very moment I rejected the opportunity of this gift of the crystal, and that was when I was a child."

"Then let us go back to that moment," Deetra said.

The old woman looked at her questioningly.

"Look into your crystal," Deetra said, "and as you do so remember the moment you received it—who gave it to you and the circumstances around the event. Call forth the memory of every detail, starting with the moment you accepted it." Deetra hesitated, watching as the woman focused her attention on the crystal. Gradually, images formed and collected about the old woman's being. To Deetra, it was like looking at picture cards fanned out in front of her to tell a story.

Estella, it seemed, had slipped away from her playmates in the meadow just above the village. It was there the old messenger approached and handed her the crystal. His words were the same words he had said to her and the same ones she had heard him say to the student Tolar. "This is a gift from the Hanta to you. What you do with it is your gift to the Hanta."

Estella had accepted the crystal and after the old messenger had gone, she hid it away in her apron pocket and returned home. Her parents met her with grievous news, saying that while she was away some ill fortune had fallen upon their family and that her little brother had been killed in an accident. Estella believed that the Hanta's gift was responsible and that the crystal was an object of bad luck and she never told anyone about it but, not knowing how to dispose of it, kept it hidden among her personal belongings. She did not take it out and look at it again until she began attending Deetra's village classes just a short time ago.

Deetra closed the old woman's hand about the crystal and cupped the closed hand between hers. "It is not too late for you," she said gently. "But you must let go of your uncertainty of whether the crystal was an instrument in your brother's death."

The old woman closed her eyes and rocked her head back and forth. "I cannot," she said. "I know that had I not received the crystal, my brother would still be alive."

"What makes you so sure?" Deetra asked.

The old woman closed her eyes, seemingly slipping from consciousness. Deetra held onto her hand and in the way she had come to know, she followed the old woman into the inner planes.

Estella was running from Deetra, desperately trying to free herself of the crystal which she still held tightly in her hand. Then suddenly she stopped running. Her body shook nervously as her eyes met Deetra's. "You are here because I asked you here," the old woman said, "and so I shall not run away. Please excuse my foolishness."

Deetra was filled with compassion. It obviously took all the old woman's strength to stand before her now. "We have all been afraid," Deetra said, "and there is no shame in admitting it. But in spite of your fear, you show great courage. You stand before me, not running any longer, in command of yourself. It is because you are now in command that I can now offer you solace."

"In what way?" Estella asked.

Deetra did not answer. There was a long moment of silence between them and in it was a new manifestation. It appeared gradually at first, yet in its gradual emergence there was great power and great gentleness. It was filled with light and its form was filled with sound as well.

The Hanta stood motionless between them, his hand outstretched to Estella. It was as though the crystal's light surrounded them and the fear which had weighed upon Estella dropped away. She smiled, looking into the Holy One's eyes, and taking his outstretched hand she joined with him. They became as one being, she yielding to him, becoming one with him.

Deetra watched and though she was not a part of the merger, she understood it. Estella had been taken across the border of the formless by the Hanta. Wherever she was, she was safe and wholly herself, and she would be gaining knowledge and strength, preparing herself to return to the world of form once more.

"She is gone," the physician said, seemingly at a distance.

Deetra returned to herself and looked up at him. "Yes," she said, "she is gone. She left with the Hanta."

Sonar smiled. "I am so very glad," he said.

There was a long pause between them and as Deetra looked on Sonar she thought of how his concern for Estella won the privilege and certainty of the same treatment at the time of his translation. Hanta would be with him.

Then Deetra remembered the village class. It was already past the hour of meeting, but she sensed that some lingered, waiting for her to arrive. And with that thought in mind, she excused herself and hurried on her way.

The village square was empty, except that seated where she normally sat was the old messenger, leaning forward on his seat, his walking stick holding up his chin. He was waiting for her.

"They've all gone," the old messenger said as their eyes met. "I told them you wouldn't be here today."

Deetra stood before him, thinking of Estella and what connection she had with the land of Nome.

"Had you followed her with the Hanta you would have known," the old messenger said. "But instead you passed up the opportunity because you felt it was no longer your business." He paused, glaring at her.

Deetra did not know what to say. It was true she had felt her task completed by summoning the Hanta to Estella's aid. She did not feel it her place to follow them. She had not even considered it.

"They were going to the land of Nome," the old messenger said, raising himself and tapping his stick lightly upon the ground. "You could have gone with them. Did you think the Hanta would give you an invitation?"

Deetra was too astounded to speak.

"The Hanta does not invite, nor does he look back to see who follows. He who follows does so because he has the gumption to follow, the desire to see where he is leading. Do you understand me?"

Deetra still could not answer.

"Never mind," the old messenger said, shifting on his feet. "Not everyone is alert enough to visit Nome and perhaps you are one who is not." Then he turned to leave.

"Wait!" Deetra called after him.

The old man stopped but did not turn around.

Deetra hesitated, unsure, recalling the old messenger's first mention of Nome and how it would be her task to visit

[66]

there. She had not wanted to do so. She was anxious for her husband's return. Yet the messenger had said that it was the way Ian would return. Why then had she not been more anxious to go?

The old messenger started to walk away.

"Please wait!" she called.

He paused again, waiting, still not looking back at her. "You are too wrapped up in yourself," he said. "You have experienced much and you have met God. Now you want to be lazy. You want to stop here and rest awhile, gloat on what you think you have achieved spiritually. Well, you do it. It matters not to me." Then he walked away.

Deetra looked after him. What the old messenger had said was true. So much had happened since Ian had left on his journey and with him soon to return she wanted nothing more than to sit back and reflect on it. She did not wish to go further before his return.

Or did she?

The old messenger was moving further and further away from her. She watched him limping heavily on his stick, wondering at his age. If he was the guise of Malitara Tatz why was he so lame? Why would the spiritual adept choose such a form to represent him? She remembered when last they had met, Malitara Tatz and herself, the feeling of realizing the God-Self, the bittersweet pain of it. It was glorious, yet overwhelming. Was that why she now backed away from continuing to Nome? Was she afraid of the feeling? Did she think it would overpower her?

Yes.

She didn't *think* it would overpower her, she *knew* it. It was the power which would consume her. The love was also the power and the magnitude of it, the both in one was unbearable to the human consciousness.

She hestitated, torn by the thoughts that had just passed through her. It was true. It was unbearable to the human consciousness, but not to the higher consciousness. The land of Nome was not for the lower nature, for the human consciousness. It was for those who had recognized the God-Self and for those who could yield to it.

Suddenly she looked up, seeing the old messenger as a faint figure disappearing over the rise and she called out to him, running to meet him.

"Please wait!" she called as she ran. But the old messenger did not acknowledge her. He continued moving over the horizon. Even so, Deetra was swift and she caught up with him.

CHAPTER 7

The old messenger did not acknowledge her presence beside him for a long while. They walked silently, until they had gone some distance outside the village and then they paused, looking back from where they had come.

The village was only faintly visible, an outline of homes against a pale blue sky.

"Why are you following me?" the old messenger asked.

Deetra was caught by the question but answered quickly. "To find the land of Nome," she said.

"It doesn't exist," the old messenger said, not looking at her.

Deetra studied the expressionless old face. Why was he trying to trick her? "It does not exist here in the physical world," she said,"but it does exist."

"Then where is it?"

"I don't know."

"Why then are you following me?"

"Because I know that you will lead me there."

"Impossible!" the old man snapped, turning to face her. "How can you think I can lead you somewhere you cannot even find yourself?"

"I just know that you can," Deetra said.

"Foolish girl, have you not paid attention to anything I have said to you?" the old messenger said, looking directly at her.

Deetra could feel the blood rise in her face and she did not answer.

"Suppose I were to tell you that I was already in the land of Nome; that right this moment while speaking with you I am there," the messenger said. "What would you make of that?"

Deetra studied the lines of the old man's face, trying to understand what he was telling her. She had realized that Nome was a place of consciousness, not a place of matter.

"That's right," he said, "Nome is my home. I dwell there all the while my body dwells here." His eyes twinkled mischievously. "Won't you come and visit me?" he asked lightly.

"I would like to," she said nervously, "but I don't understand how to do it."

"Of course you don't." He turned and started walking again.

"Where are we going?" she asked, catching up with him.

"Liether has sent word that he wishes to see me," the old messenger said.

Deetra said nothing, thinking of the name Liether and what it meant to her. It seemed that long ago she had heard that name. There was a kind of legend to it. The story of a man who lived outside the village in a small shack attended to by his mother. It was said that the man was paralyzed from the neck down and that the only powers his muscles controlled were those of facial expressions and speech. It was also said that he had a very keen mind and a memory for detail which most people did not possess. The legend she had heard was one in her childhood times and it merely referred to Liether as the *bodyless one*. There were tales of how the *bodyless one* lived through his mind; how he could adventure into the fields or marketplace purely by thinking himself there. Now, as Deetra thought of it, she understood that which as a child had been so mysterious. Liether was

Soul-travelling in his adventures, just as she or any other Askan did whenever they wanted.

Was Liether then an Askan?

"Not yet," the old messenger said, turning about to look at Deetra, "but he is well on his way. It takes some a great length of time to acquire the title. Most important is the individual's realization of his circumstances in life as being the result of personal choice." He paused, leaning on his stick, looking at Deetra. "You understand that one becomes *bodyless* as Liether did because he chooses to do so?"

Deetra nodded and turned her attention to the shack ahead of them. An old woman appeared in the doorway, wiping her hands on her apron. Then she waved.

The old messenger turned about and seeing the woman went to her, introducing Deetra briefly.

Deetra smiled at the woman, who was somewhat tired in appearance and humbly dressed.

"You are welcome." the woman said, stepping out of the way and motioning them to enter.

Deetra followed the messenger through the doorway and to a chair in a corner of the room. In it sat a motionless young man. His small thin face broke out into a broad smile at their approach.

It was Liether, the *bodyless* one.

"Thank you for responding to my call," Liether said to the old messenger reverently. "So much has happened since our last visit. I was afraid to wait any longer."

"This is the Lady Deetra," the old messenger said, motioning to her standing slightly behind and to the side of him. "She was walking with me when you called me and so she came along."

Liether nodded politely to Deetra but kept his attention on the old messenger. "My travels have changed," he said, "and I don't understand them."

"In what way?" the messenger asked, leaning on his stick attentively.

"In every way," Liether said. "I no longer move about outside my body as I had trained myself to do. It seems that I am locked within it and I can no longer move. It is horrible."

"Why horrible?" the old man asked.

"To be so confined," Liether said. "My body entraps me."

The old messenger did not answer but turned and looked about the room, walking over to some shelves above the fireplace and plucking a clay pot from them. Then he returned to face Liether. "Do you know what's in this pot?" he asked.

"That's where Mother keeps the flints to light the fire," Liether answered.

The old messenger lifted a flint from within the clay pot and held it up for both to see. Then he dropped it into the pot again. "That is correct," he said to Liether. "And do you think that the flint is confined to the pot?" he asked.

Liether appeared confused and hesitated.

"Well?" the old messenger prodded.

"It is until someone removes it from the pot," the young man said, unsure.

"Very good. But tell me, when it is removed from the pot does it still have an identity with it?" the old messenger asked, resting the pot on his walking stick while balancing it with one hand.

The young man stared at the pot for a long while. "I don't know," he said finally.

"Yes you do!" the messenger said. "You must think first and then you will know the answer."

Deetra watched, intrigued by the line of questioning, relating it to a similar experience she had had with another great spiritual adept on the causal plane, viewing an incident through a doorway between the worlds. She too had been told to think before answering.

Still Liether did not answer. He lowered his eyes as if

in thought.

"Come on!" the old messenger said impatiently, tapping the bowl on the tip of his stick. "You know the answer."

"But I don't," Liether said.

"Is there a relationship between the flint and the bowl?" the messenger asked.

"Well yes," Leither said.

"Then what is that relationship?"

"One is the vessel for the other."

"Good. And which is which?"

Liether drew in a deep breath. "The pot is the vessel for the flint."

"Good. And why is that?"

"Because it seemed like a likely container for the flint," Liether said, suddenly edgy.

"And now you've got it!"

"Got what?" Liether asked.

"It is a likely container for the flint!" the old messenger repeated.

"I don't understand."

"There is no such thing as chance or happenstance," the messenger said. "Certain choices are made and they are made because the attraction of two things is likely. But now, let us look at your situation." He paused, replacing the pot on the shelf above the fireplace. "You are discontent with your vessel?"

Liether was silent, yet the turmoil which was churning within his mind was apparent. It did not make sense that he should be content with his vessel. His body could not move him about in the world. It was no more useful than the clay pot. To have chosen it would have been foolish indeed.

The old messenger looked into him deeply and did not speak.

Liether believed that it was ill fortune that he had been

stuck with such a body. Yet he had learned to live with it. He had found a way to escape it. He could close his eyes and silently step out of his body and go anywhere at will. Often he went to the market place. He knew a great many people although they didn't know him. Sometimes he would simply sit invisibly watching as others went about their daily affairs. It had become a pastime which he had grown to enjoy. But now it was as though his one pleasure had been snatched from him.

"When you learn to be comfortable within your vessel, you will discover a great many adventures you never dreamed existed," the old messenger said, knowing his thoughts. "And you will be able to enjoy the simple pleasure of watching in the marketplace again. Only next time, you will be more aware, more ready to understand your experiences. They will have more value to you as a spiritual being."

Tears rolled down Liether's face but his eyes remained firmly on the old messenger. "I feel as though I am about to die," he said softly.

The old messenger nodded. "Only in the old consciousness," he said. "The vessel you have chosen still has much purpose in your life."

"I will never believe it," he said.

"You chose this vessel so that you could *learn to do without doing*," the old messenger said. "You have learned one facet of that lesson. You have learned to move out of your body and travel invisibly in the physical realms. Now you must learn to travel the invisible realms while consciously aware within your vessel."

"But how?" Liether asked pathetically.

"I cannot answer that," the old messenger said. "You must find your own answers."

"But my disadvantage ..."

The old messenger raised his hand for silence. "You have no disadvantage that you have not chosen to have,"

[*74*]

he said. "When you understand that statement then you can continue on with your life."

"But suppose I choose to die?" Liether asked.

The old messenger did not answer.

"It is my choice, isn't it?"

Still the old messenger did not answer.

"It's not that I don't want to live," Liether said, explaining. "It's just that I don't know how to live this life I've chosen. It is so much more difficult than most."

"Do you think you are the only one enduring difficulties?" the old messenger asked.

"You mean there is another?"

"There are many others."

Liether stared at the old messenger.

"Deetra has experienced all you are experiencing," the messenger said, motioning to her on his right.

Deetra nodded that it was true. The circumstances were different in appearance but the experiences were truly the same. "You are on your way to becoming Askan," she said, encouraging him. "It is a simple path but not an easy one. As we progress, the old ways of doing things are no longer valid. If we insist on them, sometimes they are taken from us by the inner master, the Hanta, so that we may continue. We cannot progress as long as we hold onto the old way of doing things." She smiled in understanding. "At least we are never alone," she said.

Tears again filled Liether's eyes. "I wish I could believe that," he said.

"Have you ever called on the Hanta for assistance?" she asked.

"No."

"Well I have ... many, many times," she said, "and I find that when practicing the presence of the master, the inner master known as the Hanta, the answers come to me as the questions form within my mind."

"How do you do it?" Liether asked.

"Daily contemplation," Deetra continued. "Place your attention on the spiritual eye while softly chanting the HU. It takes practice, daily practice, but the rewards are there."

"Then my answers will come in this way?" Liether asked.

"Yes," Deetra said, nodding and turning to the old messenger for reinforcement, but he was gone.

The old messenger had disappeared.

Deetra turned to Liether who appeared equally surprised. "I suppose he felt he was no longer needed," Deetra said, lightly.

Liether turned his head and looked about the room as if expecting to see the old messenger.

"He had business elsewhere," Deetra said.

"But he did not even say goodbye," Liether said, his eyes touching on Deetra and then lighting about the room again. "Surely we should have seen him go."

Deetra studied the anxiety on the man's face. He was worried and concerned because of the appearance of something he didn't understand—the old messenger's disappearance. Yet it was nothing. Although she could not as yet accomplish the feat herself, she had known the old messenger to do it on numerous occasions.

"Are you an Askan?" Liether asked her.

Deetra nodded. "Yes," she said, "and now I too must be on my way."

Liether stared at her, half expecting her to disappear as the old messenger had done.

Deetra smiled. "I will leave by the door," she said lightly, "and with your permission I will return to visit you again."

"Please do," Liether said enthusiastically.

"I haven't many to talk with, only Mother."

"Then I will see you soon," she said, waving to him and acknowledging his mother who sat sewing across the room.

Then she left.

CHAPTER 8

Deetra walked slowly back to the sanctuary, wondering if she had failed once again. The old messenger had gone and left her with Liether. Had she again missed an opportunity to enter the land of Nome?

Did she leave Liether too soon?

Did being with him present an opportunity she could not see?

She thought not.

She understood Liether's situation. He had created the karma for his choice to be immobile and now he was living the drama like a player on stage. They were all living their dramas—herself, the physician Sonar, Estella, Liether, Tolar, the old messenger and Malitara Tatz as well.

The thought startled her.

But why?

It was not the first time she had considered life as players upon a stage. It was an old analogy, one which they had tossed about as youngsters when trying to appear profound. But now an unidentified feeling crept out of the analogy and moved toward her. It was so plain, so visible that she could not at first see it.

Its visiblility was so ordinary. It was subtle.

What she was seeing was simply herself as the lead actor in her own play. She had written the script and staged it, even chosen the players to play opposite her.

Nome was of her own making.

Or was it?

The old messenger had introduced her to the search for

Nome. Yet the old messenger was merely acting out his role in her play.

Could it be so?

The realizaiton enveloped her as though a sleeve had been slipped over her world, blocking out everything else. There in her sightless gaze she saw a tiny image of herself. It was the same image she had seen in Malitara Tatz's eyes, only this time the image was in limbo, unsupported by any physical form and instead of looking back at her, she was observing it.

The tiny image of herself appeared to be seated, gazing into space and pondering deeply on the matters she now realized.

Why was she seeing herself in this way?

Then it struck her.

She was seeing an image of her consciousness; the reflection of it seated somewhere in the inbetween worlds, planes of existence within the invisible realms. She was not seeing her physical form but a reflection of it impressed on the ethers; impressed on the all-pervading life force, on the *force* itself. She had achieved such sight by maintaining a certain detachment. She could not explain it to herself without losing it, but it was there. It was real enough. The image and its colors were slightly softer, as she would have expected a reflection to be.

Then she saw something else.

The tiny image of herself also had a reflection and next to it was still another reflection and another, each softer and fainter than the one before it.

She counted.

There were five reflections which were distinct but many more beyond which were too faint to discern.

There were five visible images of herself.

What did they mean?

Instantly she knew.

Each reflection represented a distinct level of consciousness. The more distinct the reflection, the closer it was to her physical world. The less distinct the reflection, the more God-like it was. And each reflection had a distinct sound which seemed to radiate from it. The coarsest was nearest the physical—thunder, bells, running water and buzzing bees. It became finer and finer as the reflection faded into its own light. She recognized a thin high-pitched sound as the melody she had claimed as her own. It appeared in the realm of fainter God-like reflections. Beyond, where the five reflections ended, there came a humming sound and the sound of the wind, only there was no wind. All the sounds were distinct but they were also one with each other. Together they played a strange, alluring music, so haunting that Deetra completely forgot herself in it.

She was *there*.

She was in *it*.

She was *it*.

The images merged to disappear in an explosion of light and sound. Deetra heard the dimensions of the musical spheres; had recognized herself as a part of *IT*, and now *IT* encompassed her. No longer did she think of herself as the human form, yet human was now a term she truly understood. She was HUMAN, not woman or man, but HU-man. She was part of the great form without form, the HU, the voice of SUGMAD, the God of gods. And in the light and sound she recognized the *all* through nothingness and nothingness through the *all*. She was alone but not alone. With her was everything and nothing.

She could not feel her body.

She could not hear her mind.

She was suspended somewhere in limbo, in a nothingness that was both light and sound, a form without form, an entity which existed, a total *being* which was *beingless*.

"Nome is consciousness," the nothingness pulsed. "It is not your consciousness, but THE consciousness and you are a part of it." Suddenly there was utter stillness and the stillness seemed to roll back, unfolding itself into more stillness, absolute and extraordinary. There was not a sound.

"Who are you?" a voice seemed to call out.

Deetra was shocked by the power of it and hesitated, collecting herself. "I am the HU in man form," she heard herself answer.

"And do you have a name?" the voice asked again, yet it was not a voice but an impulse or a wave of energy directed at her.

Deetra considered the question, knowing that her identity was all identities. She was all the images, all the reflections she had known. She was a part of the HU in man form but she was also without the mankind form. She was the HU *itself,* the consciousness. THE CONSCIOUSNESS.

The realization struck her, tore at her and seemingly ripped her, limb from limb, as though tearing her apart. It ripped at her until she yielded, *knowing* she was truly the form without form. Somehow she was part of *it* and the consciousness of *it* was Nome. *There was only one beingness!*

She was in Nome!

She was IT!

The deep utter silence of Nome enveloped her. It was empty silence, yet powerful with the force of love and she felt hugged by it. It was complete, the height of beingness and it was something else. She found herself moving toward this something, as though trying to grasp it and as she did, the silence rolled back and gradually she became aware of her human form once again.

She opened her eyes.

She was lying on her back on the side of the path which led to the sanctuary. Then she recalled that she had been on her way home when ...

She stopped herself from thinking and raised herself to her feet.

Deetra never felt more alone. No one had acknowledged her presence as she had entered the sanctuary and now that she was within her private chambers she knew that she was meant to be alone.

There was nothing to think about, only again and again she recalled her peculiar entrance into Nome and each time the memory was drawn she became more aware of a great change which had taken place within her.

The change was accompanied by a deep longing. Deetra knew the feeling from previous experiences she had had, only now the longing severed her feelings from the physical world. There was nothing in the world of matter which seemed to hold her attention. She did not care if her body died, nor did she care if the bodies of others died. The physical world was a mere reflection and it seemed puny and lifeless next to other higher worlds of SUGMAD.

CHAPTER 9

Deetra envisioned herself shut up alone for days in her chamber until Ian's return but it did not work out that way. The following day there was a light but determined rap at her door. She moved slowly across the room and absently opened it.

The physician Sonar stood restlessly in the doorway. "You are needed at the Village Square," he said anxiously. "Will you come right away?"

Deetra studied the man. She had grown accustomed to the deep concerned lines that had been etched into his face. As village physician he would always be caught in the concerns of others. "What is happening at the square?" she asked.

"A man in pink robes is there trying to win the affection of your class."

Deetra was caught by surprise. She had forgotten about her class; had not given it the slightest thought since last she had attended, only to find the old messenger waiting for her with the news that he had dismissed the class for the day. And now a man in pink robes was there in place of her. Could it be that she had been replaced by the Pink Prince, Lord Casmir, the negative force. "Let us go," she said. "You can tell me what you know on the way."

They were hurrying across the sanctuary grounds when Sonar said, "The man in pink was there when I arrived this noon. I was late but not very, yet already the class had settled down and was listening to what the man was saying."

"And what was he saying?" Deetra asked without stopping.

"He was telling those present about the law of opposites and about how the negative force overpowers the positive in the physical worlds," Sonar said, hesitating.

"Go on," Deetra said, prodding.

"He was telling them that to yield to the negative force was merely to yield to the flow of physical life, and that it was the way to happiness and contentment. He said that negative did not mean bad any more than positive meant good." The physician hesitated again, catching his breath. "He was also telling them that in yielding to the flow of physical life that he would establish a bond of affection between each of them that was indestructible; that the bond meant total happiness and sheer bliss."

"Dear Hanta!" Deetra called out. She stopped walking, looking past the physician who was watching her.

"Do you know this man in pink robes?" Sonar asked.

Deetra nodded without speaking, but the seriousness etched on her face said it all to Sonar.

"I came to get you," he said, "because something within told me that the man was destructive. I don't know why, but I knew that I had to get help."

"You were right to do so," Deetra said, thinking that if she had not forgotten to attend her class the negative force could not have entered. Then she checked the thought, knowing that those in attendance had to have been strong in order to attract the interest of so strong a negative force. "What the man in pink robes said about the law of opposites was true," Deetra said, "but what he did not say was that they do not exist outside of the lower worlds."

"The lower worlds?" the physician asked.

"Our next class lesson," Deetra said, turning about. "Let us continue on our way."

[*83*]

As they approached the square there was a low murmuring sound, exclamations of awe as if some spectacular feat had been performed. Sonar led the way, stepping back to let Deetra move to the center of the class. All eyes were averted, turning toward her.

Deetra looked about the square. There was no one in pink robes. There were only those she had come to know on a personal basis, those who had been in daily attendance to her class.

"What has happened?" Sonar asked, turning about in surprise.

But Deetra knew. It struck her as quickly as the eyes of the class reached out to her. The man in pink had disappeared the moment she neared the square. It was the disappearance of the negative force in lieu of the approaching positive. As an Askan she had great power and she did not have to purposefully exercise it. She need only present herself in a situation. Deetra was a carrier for the Divine Force, a channel through which it could flow and her movement about the village changed it and the situations occurring by her very presence.

Did the villagers know?

She thought not.

"What has happened here?" the physician called out once again. "Where is the man in pink robes? Is he still among you?"

Deetra touched the physician lightly on the arm.

He turned to her.

"It is all right," she said softly.

The physician looked about, confused. The others looked at one another and took their places on the stone benches, as though they had risen only to greet the Lady Deetra.

Deetra moved to her accustomed place and sat down. She waited until Sonar too was seated and the others grew quiet. "I am sorry that I was late," Deetra said. "You may have wondered where I've been these last few days and I appreciate your eagerness to learn. These last days I have been preoccupied with my own lessons, lessons reflected here but also taking place on another plane of existence." She paused, searching the faces of those in front of her. Sonar was intense and did not move. The others were equally intense and seemed to hang onto her every word. Then she saw Tolar seated on the grass off to the side of the class. As the others, his expression clung to her. She called to him.

"Tolar, would you come forward and sit next to me?" she asked, patting a length of stone bench next to her.

The man rose and came hesitantly toward her. Then he sat down where she had requested.

Deetra smiled.

Instantly Tolar was put at ease.

"Would you tell me and the class what you've seen here today," she asked.

Their eyes met and then Tolar lowered his.

"Please," she said softly, encouragingly.

Tolar looked up at her and then addressed the class. "We had a visitor today," he said, hesitating, "an unusual looking man dressed in pink robes who spoke to us about the law of opposites and how the law could work for us." He stopped and turned to Deetra.

"Please go on," she said.

Tolar looked up at her and then addressed the class. "He also told us that the negative force was the powerful force in our daily lives and that to yield to it was to yield to our most powerful nature." Tolar hesitated again. "In essence, that is all," he said. "The rest were examples of how the negative force provides; and then you came in." He looked at Deetra.

"What happened when I came in?" Deetra asked, prodding.

"The man in pink disappeared," Tolar said.

[85]

A low whispering went through the class, the same whispering Deetra had heard when she first approached with Sonar. She waited for it to die down before she asked Tolar what he made of the situation.

Tolar shrugged his shoulders. The others laughed, except for the physician.

"Sonar came to fetch me," Deetra said, explaining. "He came to the sanctuary because he believed there was something peculiar happening."

"There was something peculiar happening all right," Tolar said.

The others laughed again.

"What did you find peculiar?" Deetra asked Tolar.

Tolar started to speak and then caught himself.

"Please speak up," Deetra said. "It is important for everyone, including yourself."

"The man in pink knew every one of us," Tolar said, uneasily. "He called each one of us by name."

"And you never met him before today?" Deetra asked.

"No."

"Are you sure?"

"Quite sure."

"Was there nothing about him that was familiar?" she asked again.

"No," he said thoughtfully. "I'm sure of it."

Deetra turned to the others in the class. "And is there no one here who recognized our visitor?" she asked.

There was a sudden silence as she looked from face to face for a reaction. A child waved his arm behind some adults and then wiggled his way into the foreground.

"I know the man," the child said, coming forward. "He is my friend."

A low murmur broke through the class. It sounded like the wind on a stormy day. Deetra reached her hand out to the child and the boy came closer, taking it.

He was a small boy, perhaps five or six, with tiny

hands that gripped Deetra tightly. Deetra looked into his frail face. It showed no fear, yet there was a certain strain in it which cautioned her.

"What is your name?" she asked.

"Pruit," the boy said.

"And you say you know the man in pink robes?" she asked slowly.

"Uhhhh," the boy said.

"You say you are friends?" Deetra asked.

"He is my good friend," Pruit said. "We play together every day."

Deetra looked deeply into the boy. His grip tightened on her fingers, his tiny hand digging into her flesh. "Do you know who I am?" she asked.

"I know," Pruit said, smiling. "Do you know who I am?"

The boy's eyes flashed under her gaze.

She knew who he was. Pruit was not a child of the village. He had no mother in her class. He was a child in strength next to hers but should she suddenly leave, he would be no child at all.

"Tell us of your games with the man in pink robes," Deetra instructed.

The child turned to face the others and grinned. "We visit people," he said, "and we play with people."

"In what way?"

"In every way." The boy turned to face her again, grinning. "You want me to say something so that all will know," he said. "Don't you?"

"If you wish."

Tolar suddenly jumped from his seat next to Deetra and moved back among the others. A kind of movement went through the class, one looking at the other without speaking.

Suddenly the boy let go of Deetra's hand and turned to the class, his hands on his hips. "My name is Pruit," he said, confidentially, "and I am a friend of the man in pink robes because.. " He stopped, looking at the adults in front of him, grinning broadly, "because we are alike."

"In what way?" Deetra again prodded.

"We are alike in every way," Pruit answered, without turning to look at her.

There was a long moment of silence, then Deetra rose from her seat, standing next to the boy. He was little taller than her knees. "Who in this class has a crystal?" she asked.

Slowly hands were raised, first one, then another, and another. Everyone in the class had a crystal.

"How many are on journey to the City of Light?" Deetra asked again.

Hesitantly all hands went up again. Deetra was pleased. She knew that although those in her class had had crystals for many years, it was only recently that they began to exercise them. They had just begun their journey.

"If you have your crystal with you, withdraw it and hold it up to the light in front of you," she instructed. She purposely did not look down at Pruit who was mimicking her at her side.

In a moment the square was alive with crystals raised high above each head. A rainbow array of light danced about the semi-circle of stone benches.

"Now look into your crystal's light," Deetra instructed, "and notice what you see there."

There was a gasp from one and the sound of it multiplied. "It's the man in pink," someone called out. "It's the boy. He's the man in pink robes!"

The boy Pruit chuckled, otherwise unmoved by the class.

"Maintain your attention on the image in the crystal," Deetra instructed again, "but as you do so sing the word HU. I will start. You all pick it up and sing with me," She began, "HUuuuuuu ... HUuuu ... HUuuuuuu." Everyone in the class began to sing the word. A moment later they all stopped, astonished.

The boy Pruit was gone.

"What has happened?" the physician asked, hurrying to his feet and coming forward.

Deetra sat down again on the stone bench. "What do you think has happened?" she asked, throwing the question back at him.

Sonar appeared puzzled and turned away.

"Think now," Deetra said, "what has happened here?"

"The song of HU chased the boy away," a woman called out.

Deetra glanced in the direction of the woman but said nothing. She felt it necessary that those present realize for themselves what had happened and how.

"Yes, it was the HU," another called out.

"He will never come again," another said.

"That's not so," Tolar said, rising to his feet.

"How do you know?" the person asked.

"I know because I am constantly confronted by him," Tolar said, facing the group.

"Why didn't you say you knew the boy when Deetra asked?" someone called out.

"Because I didn't recognize the boy, nor did I recognize the man in pink robes," Tolar said, "but now I understand that there are many disguises for the negative force— one was a woman who stole my crystal. The negative force assumes many roles. To succeed on the path we must learn to recognize the force as it presents itself in our lives." He paused and turned to Deetra. "I am so grateful to at last understand this fact," he said.

"I too have met this force in many disguises," she said. "We all have, but it is not until we recognize the presence of the force—both negative and positive—that they are of any value to us."

"Why did you include the positive force in that statement?" Tolar asked.

[*89*]

"Because one is born of the other," Deetra said.

Tolar sat down and looked at her quizzically, waiting for an explanation.

"The negative is born of the positive," Deetra said, explaining, "but the negative force only exists in the lower worlds, the worlds of matter, feeling and thought." She paused, studying the faces of those about her. The class seemed intensely interested.

"All of what the man in pink robes told you was true," she said, starting again, "that is, about the law of opposites existent in the lower worlds. And the negative force is more predominant in the worlds of matter. There is instant happiness, as the man in pink said, when one is in tune with the negative force." She paused. A low murmuring went through the class. "But what he didn't tell you was that the instant happiness only lives for an instant because the negative force is constantly building desires within us and these desires breed discontent." Deetra paused again. "Are there any questions?" she asked.

"Yes," the physician said, "then what is the answer?"

"The higher you rise on the spiritual scale, the more aware you become of the subtleties of life, and the less you are under the control of the negative force. In all actuality, you saw the negative force diminish in front of you this day," Deetra said. "You saw a man diminish to the size of a boy and you saw the boy fade out completely as the vibration of HU dominated. So you see, as powerful as the negative force is in the physical world of matter, it is still subordinate to the positive force."

"It doesn't appear that way to me," Sonar the physician said. "Every day I see suffering triumphing."

"And what does that mean to you?" Deetra asked.

"That the negative force is stronger," Sonar said.

Deetra studied the physician, understanding, then began, "As the God-force filters down from SUGMAD, it changes. For one thing the Divine Force produces sounds and the sounds take one form nearest the SUGMAD and another form nearest the physical world. It is like the notes on a musical scale. It is the descending sound from SUG-MAD which creates matter or that which produced the physical world. This lower vibration or sound is what we call the negative force, but actually it is nothing more than the positive force in lower vibration.

"If one focused his attention on the lower vibration what happens?" Deetra asked, glancing from face to face.

No one answered.

"The lower vibration is the Force, the Divine Force, so dense that it is made manifest," Deetra said, pausing to look into the faces of those about her. "In other words, we are talking about the negative force."

She stopped talking as though waiting for someone to answer, but no one did.

"If one focuses his attention on the negative force," Deetra said once again, "he or she attracts the attentions of those negative forces. One then becomes touched by the negative in all aspects of his or her life and becomes the effect of negativity. And now here is the clue! If instead, one focuses attention on the positive forces, the higher vibrations of SUGMAD, then he begins to become aware of the presence of the negative as a natural part of life but no longer is affected by it. He begins to take control of his own life. An Askan is merely one who has become aware and who has taken control of his or her own life."

"You mean the negative ceases to exist for the Askan?" Tolar asked, raising himself on his haunches as he spoke.

"No. In the lower worlds or physical worlds the negative always exists," Deetra said, "but to an Askan the negative is no longer bad. He is controller of his own fate. He lives in the negative world but he is not of it. He is the cause but not the effect."

She rose from her seat. "You have all experienced much this day," she said. "We will close here so that you can contemplate on what has taken place. Go to that temple within and seek understanding there. We will meet again when the Hanta returns."

Mention of the Hanta caused an immediate stir and, as Deetra turned and walked out of the square, she heard whispering of comments about the Hanta by those in the class.

CHAPTER 10

Deetra awoke to a rap on her chamber door. She sat up just as the old messenger stepped into the room.

"I am on my way to meet the Hanta," he said. "If you would like to join me, you may."

"When are you leaving?" Deetra asked, sleepily.

"As soon as you are ready," he said.

She rose to her feet, pulling her nightgown closely about herself and folded her arms about her chest. "I will be ready directly," she said.

The old messenger nodded and left the room. As she dressed, Deetra considered the old messenger's return to her chamber. She had not seen him for some days. Then she thought of Ian. Was she joining the old man to meet with her husband or with the Hanta. He had said the Hanta, yet she wondered if she would be able to separate the two, or if she needed to do so.

The old messenger quietly led the way through the village, across the wheat fields to the mountain range on the far side. Then he looked up towards the top, raising his walking staff and motioning to it. "We will meet the Hanta on the summit," he said.

Deetra scanned the ridge. It was the highest mountain in the range. It would not be an easy climb and she was doubtful if it could be accomplished in a single day without any supplies.

"I have done it," the old messenger said, leaning upon his staff, studying her. "Is there any reason you cannot?"

Deetra looked to the wrinkled old face. She envisioned the old man limping up the mountain, wondering if Malitara Tatz maintained that guise to mock her. Yet, as she looked into his eyes, she felt a warm glow of love pouring from them into her. "I can make it," she answered.

The old man nodded, then turned away. He placed his staff in front of him and, using it to lean upon, he began to walk up the mountain. Deetra looked after him. He was at first the old messenger and then, as he moved ahead of her, he transformed. Only his walking staff was the same. It was no longer the old messenger leading her, but Malitara Tatz who led the way. They did not speak, but continued steadily rising up the side of the mountain, until finally Malitara Tatz stopped and turned to face her.

Deetra was badly out of breath and looked up, smiling, grateful for the pause.

Malitara Tatz's expression was sober. "Why are you resisting?" he asked seriously.

Deetra was surprised by the question and did not answer. She had not thought herself to be resisting. She had not considered it. She lowered her eyes, suddenly aware that the spiritual adept was breathing normally and seemingly not in the least fatigued.

"Why are you resisting this journey?" he asked again.

At the question Deetra looked into the serious but kindly face. "I don't know," she said. "I didn't realize until this moment that I was resisting."

"There is no point in trying to continue," Tatz said, "you'll never make it."

The two looked at each other, waiting. Deetra knew that the adept was waiting for her to explain herself but she did not know what to say.

"Your mind is split and it tugs against you," Malitara Tatz said. "Why?"

Deetra shook her head but did not speak.

"You know!" the adept shot back.

Deetra wanted to look away, to run back down the mountainside but she felt held to the spot, not by the adept but by a part of herself. She wanted to continue and yet she did not.

"You cannot move in two directions," Malitara Tatz said softly.

Deetra nodded. "I know," she said.

"Then look at your resistance and recognize it. Recognition itself has the power to free you if you so choose."

Deetra lowered her eyes. She felt ashamed of the feeling which was rising in her. "It's just that it seems I've been this way so many times," she said. "First there was the journey to Moonwalk where I encountered the negative force, and then there was the mountain of light and the doorways between the worlds. I have experienced the astral and the causal planes. I know them in detail. I know that beyond them there is only Soul and SUGMAD. But instead I am climbing a mountain again, once more adventuring, but this time the adventure seems pointless." She drew in a deep breath. "I feel there is nothing more for me to learn." Her last words fell from her with tremendous weight and she felt paralyzed by the heaviness.

Malitara Tatz stood looking at her. His face was expressionless but his eyes held great compassion. "And so you wish to stay where you are," he said.

"It's not that."

"Then what?"

"It all seems so unnecessary," she said.

"The effort?"

"Yes."

"You have realized self as Soul and you have realized God and so you think there is nothing more," Malitara Tatz said.

"I'm sure there is more," Deetra said.

"But you see no point to anything more," the adept said. "Is that it?"

"Yes, I suppose it is," Deetra said.

"And the Hanta?"

"You mean my husband Ian?"

"I mean your husband Ian who is the Hanta," Malitara Tatz said. "Did you think yourself equal to that consciousness?"

"Of course not," she said, "but I am equal to Ian the man."

"Ian the man and the Hanta are inseparable," the adept said. "You knew when your marriage took place that you were marrying no ordinary man. Your marriage cannot endure stagnation."

"You mean I must choose," Deetra said.

"Yes," Malitara Tatz said sadly.

Deetra fought a sudden urge to run away. There was nowhere to run. If she did not allow her husband, the Hanta consciousness, to fill her life, then her life was over. She had hit a plateau and was comfortable there, yet the comfort was illusionary because it was locked in a world of time and space.

It was time and space she had mastered, not the planes of Soul. She had come into a state of control over her physical life and the psychic energies reaching into it. She was free and detached from the things of the world, from emotion and from illusions of thought—yet . . . She looked into the adept's kindly face and in his eyes she once again saw a tiny image of herself. A rush of joy went through her as suddenly, without thought, she realized that a great moment was being relived. She was seeing herself in the adept and she was seeing through his eyes.

But what she was seeing was herself locked in a prison of her own making. She had reached a certain height of spiritual awareness and was satisfied with it. She had vision to see through life's illusions and the power to deal with them. She had arrived at a place far beyond her expectations. She had knowledge now that she never before realized existed. What else was there?

As she looked at herself through the adept's eyes, a peculiar thing happened. She was herself looking at the adept. As she looked into him she saw that he was fully aware of her, yet as Soul there was no distinction between the two of them. They were one and the same and yet individual. And then she saw what their individuality was.

Malitara Tatz possessed a realization and experience far beyond hers. Deetra's was a conquering of mind and passion, and she had the power in the worlds of thought and imagination. Malitara Tatz was beyond these. He worked and lived in a realm beyond thought and imagination and, although she caught a glimpse of it, she could not say what it was she saw. It was all light, brilliant white light and the perfect music of HU. Was this what the adept had meant about dwelling in the land of Nome?

Her question once formed separated her consciousness from the adept's. She looked at him now as herself looking at any man, yet distinctly aware of who he was. The question rose in her again: *Was this what the adept had meant about dwelling in the land of Nome?*

"Yes," Malitara Tatz said softly, smiling. "Now you see!"

Deetra paused within herself, listening to the single high-pitched sound of Soul, the Divine Force which linked her to SUGMAD. Inwardly she clung to it. It was all and everything to her, only now she knew that there was more, a refinement of the sound. How would she achieve it?

Slowly, gradually in the melody which was her own, she realized that she would have to release her mental grip on that sound, set her image of it free so that it could return to her in another form.

But could she?

She was afraid of losing herself; of losing her center and her control. It was ridiculous, of course, but neverthe-less a fact. How could she give up the sound which had guided her so perfectly through the lower planes?

Deetra looked at Malitara Tatz once again and saw that he knew her thoughts.

"The Hanta is with you always," the spiritual adept said. "You need to fear nothing."

How well she knew and how well she knew she knew. She had drilled that knowledge into the village students; had taken their hands so to speak and led them to the God-man. And now it was she who was being coddled. The teacher was the student. Would it never end?

Malitara Tatz gently touched her shoulder and smiled. "I too am a student," he said, "and so is the Hanta. It never ends and if ever we find that it does, we know as individuals we have refused to go higher. We have then accepted the pitiful state of stagnation, or spiritual inertia. Do you understand me?"

Deetra was steadily gazing at him and she nodded. "Thank you," she said, drawing in a deep breath. "And now I feel ready to continue the journey."

The journey upward was easier for Deetra now that she had resigned herself to continue but it was not joyous. Something was missing. She distinctly had the feeling of being alone, of wandering so to speak. Frequently her inner senses called out to her, begging for information on what was ahead, and always the calling was answered with suspicion and uncertainty. And she felt ashamed. Occasionally, she glanced at Malitara Tatz as he walked ahead of her, wondering what the magnificent being had in store for her. But her wonderings were not answered. The adept moved ahead silently, leaving her to herself.

Then she had an idea.

With all her mental strength she shifted her attention to behold the land of Nome. She recalled the image of herself in Malitara Tatz's eyes, of being one with him, of seeing through his eyes to his inner being—that moment when she caught a glimpse of Nome within him and that intense light and sound.

At first it eluded her. Over and over again she recalled the memory of his beingness and then, as if quite unexpectedly, she caught it. The memory became an image and the image a reality. Suddenly she was within the moment.

The light was blinding.

Malitara Tatz reached for her hand and took it, guiding her through the blinding brilliance. They were moving to somewhere, although everywhere there was intense light, so white and bright it almost appeared solid. And in it no manner of form could be ascertained. Although Deetra could feel the warmth of the spiritual adept's hand in her own, she could not see him and she could no longer see herself.

They stopped walking and in something like telepathy Malitara Tatz told her to remain where she was until his return. Then he let go of her hand and departed.

Deetra stood motionless, barely breathing, if at all. The white light seemed to have entered her and taken her body over. She was no longer her physical self, but *it* , the light, and yet she had consciousness within *it*.

It spoke to her, not in words but in a pulsing communication which throbbed in and through her.

"Do you know who I am?" the voice asked.

"You are the consciousness of Nome," Deetra answered in like communication.

"Which is?" it asked.

"Myself." Deetra was surprised by her answer. It was not anything she had thought about or concluded. In the moment she was asked, her innermost being responded, yet it was only now that her human consciousness realized the fact. Soul was the consciousness of Nome. She was Soul. She was that consciousness. It was Soul who had answered the questioner.

[*99*]

"If both you and I are the consciousness of Nome, then who are we?" the voice asked again.

Deetra had already begun to think and therefore spontaneity eluded her. She did not answer.

There was a moment of utter silence. It was so extraordinary, so complete that she became lost in it. The silence seemed to become fuller and fuller, like a bubble, and then it burst into beautiful music.

The music was thin and fine, unlike any heard by the physical senses. And it was not exteriorized but interiorized. It moved through her as naturally as the air she breathed, and it nourished her as well. Then it too became fuller and fuller, so intense that it burst like a spark into flame, and suddenly the light was dimmed and the music humanly audible. She could see herself, the form of the terrain about her and just ahead was Malitara Tatz, watching her.

She was standing on the side of the mountain with Malitara Tatz.

She looked at him questioningly

"We had best be on our way," he said, motioning to the distance still remaining to the top of the mountain. Then he turned and started toward the summit.

Although Deetra followed, she was still caught by the question which had eluded her within the brilliant white light. A voice had asked: *"If both you and I are the consciousness of Nome, then who are we?"* Over and over again she rolled the question over in her mind and seemingly, each time she became more confused and more uncertain. If she had answered in a moment without thinking she might have said something like *then we are the Soul of Nome,* but she knew that it would not be satisfactory. It was true, of course, she and the voice were the Soul of Nome, but what was Nome?

Her eyes were on the ground, watching where Malitara Tatz chose his steps and she followed in them. The adept never stumbled and his gait was light and easy to follow.

The episode reminded her of following Ian up the mountain toward Moonwalk when first she had started her conscious journey to SUGMAD seemingly long ago. It was when she had first come to realize that following the spiritual path was made easier by following an experienced traveller. And so this time it was Malitara Tatz. For all her knowledge and experience she still required an adept to guide her.

She thought of her marriage to Ian who was now the Hanta. How could she have come so far and still be so dependent? How was she worthy of being wife to Hanta?

The question faded almost as soon as it arose. She had no real question regarding the love bond between her and her husband. Their union was the height of all unions and she knew herself to be equal to it or else it could not have been.

What was the consciousness of Nome?

Malitara Tatz stopped, motioning with his hand as he did so. He seemed to be listening for something. Then he turned to face her and in a low voice said, "Wait here. I shall return shortly."

Deetra stood motionless, surprised. She had the distinct feeling she was about to repeat an experience. She wanted to mention it to Malitara Tatz, but he raised his index finger to his lips, indicating silence, quickly turned, walked up over the rise and disappeared.

Looking about, Deetra chose a rock and sat down. She felt herself to be such a neophyte. She knew that she was climbing the summit to take the next step in her spiritual unfoldment, yet she did not know what it was or what she could do to speed herself along. She was like a child reaching out into life for the first time.

Inwardly she began to chant the HU, calling on the Hanta to point the way to her. She spoke to him as both husband and Hanta, as both friend and adept, and in her inward whispers she told him of her love.

It was then that a peculiar question formed itself within

her. *Was Nome life?*

No. It was the consciousness of life.

Or could it be the essence of life?

No. It was the creator of the essence. It was the power behind it.

What then was Nome?

The answer came, not in words, but in something far beyond. It was a perception of sorts, a formless awareness of an existence beyond imagination and thought. And yet it had the power to manifest in form. She was living proof of it. The environment about her proved it as well. As the power filtered down from the high, it formed reflection and the reflection was form. It took form. She was *IT*. The environment was *IT*. Malitara Tatz was *IT*. The Hanta was *IT*. All being *IT, IT* was all. The consciousness of Nome was *IT* and *IT* was Deetra and *IT* was the All. *IT* was the SUGMAD, the Endless One and all beings and things reflected *IT*.

Deetra was a reflection of SUGMAD.

It struck her with more impact than any feeling she had ever known. And in that moment she had total awareness of herself, and yet she was without physical feeling at all. She had detached herself from her body and now stood outside it, looking at it, feeling love and reverence for the keen reflection animated to experience the meaning of life. Her body was part of that experience!

Life was the experience! Yet it was merely a series of experiences whereby one may recognize similarities between nature and self and finally realizing that self was Soul. At that point one begins to be a co-worker with SUGMAD and through service recognize *its oneness with it*.

The inner vision was interrupted by sounds from the summit. There were voices, seemingly many of them and, when she looked up, she saw faces peering down at where she sat.

She stood up.

She recognized no one.

"Who is there?" she called out.

"Come and see," one called back.

Deetra stood, staring up into the faces peering down at her. There was something strangely familiar about them, although she didn't know why. "Who is there?" she called again.

"Don't you recognize us?" one called back.

Deetra strained to get a glimpse of the speaker, yet she was sure she did not know who it was. She wondered if Malitara Tatz was among them but something within her rejected the idea. She could not envision the spiritual adept a party to such a comical scene.

"We've been waiting for you, Deetra," the same one called out.

She looked from face to face, all smiling approval. "And why have you been waiting?" Deetra asked the one who had spoken.

"To take you to Nome," the one said, grinning. "You did want to go there?"

Deetra was astonished and did not answer. Of course, she had wanted to go to Nome, and she had been there. Why did these peculiar-looking figures believe they could assist her? Who or what were they?

"You can't get to Nome without first meeting us," the voice said.

"But I have been there," Deetra said softly to herself.

"You have only been to the gateway, but you have not passed through it," the one said, as if answering her. "If you wish to go through, you must meet us."

Deetra turned away and looked down the mountain. Something within her wanted to run, to escape but it was ridiculous. There was nothing to escape.

Or was there?

Malitara Tatz had told her to wait; that he would return shortly, and she remembered how she had been lost in thought when he motioned her to be silent. He had seemed to be listening to something. Then he left. Had he heard those who now looked down on her from the summit?

Deetra looked up. The still grinning faces peered over the cliff, looking down upon her as if waiting.

"Is Malitara Tatz there with you?" she asked.

"Yes, yes he is," the one answered.

"Will you ask him to come to the edge of the cliff?" Deetra asked. "I should like to speak with him."

"Can't do it!" the one said emphatically."

Deetra felt a deep sense of caution but decided to probe further. She had no telepathic communication with this being, nor any of the others who watched silently. "And why not?" she asked.

"Because we won't let him," the one said.

"You won't let him," Deetra repeated. She did not think it likely that the spiritual adept could be controlled by such a crew. "Call him at once." Then Deetra called him inwardly, using a form of communication which only Askans can use with one another, and she told the adept of the peculiar people-like beings peering at her from the top of the mountain and asked for his guidance on the situation.

"He is occupied," the one grinning from above said, "but if you will join us, he will be free in short order."

Deetra considered the offer, cautioned by the memory of Malitara Tatz asking her to wait. "Who are you?" she asked again.

"Surely you recognize at least one of us," the one said.

Deetra looked hard at the one who spoke, moving a few steps up the mountain to have a closer glimpse. His features, or *its* features, were not familiar at all, in that the person, if it was a person, was not anyone she recognized. But there was something in the general countenance of the individual which struck her. Suddenly the face stopped grinning and turned as if to motion attention to the others with it.

One by one Deetra looked at them. Each was distinctly different from the other, yet each bore a resemblence to the leader. It wasn't in features that they resembled one another, but something else; something in magnetism; something in retrospect to each other; something which was difficult to pinpoint but definitely apparant to the beholder.

Then it struck her.

It was not their similarities to each other which were so profound, but in some way to herself. They seemed to be bits of her.

In what way?

Again she studied the faces of those above her. They in no way resembled her. They were sexless, so to speak, each bearing a prominent feature. One had a large nose, another seemingly huge lips, another enormous ears, another had eyes which bulged and the speaker was peculiar too, but in a different way. He or she had no prominent features; everything was well proportioned and its skin appeared smooth. It wasn't the exterior of the person which was peculiar, but the interior. As Deetra looked from face to face, she wondered what the rest of them looked like; if they had bodies; if indeed they were human.

"We cannot come to you," the one called down to her. "If you wish to pass into Nome you will have to come to us."

Deetra turned her attention to the high-pitched sounds of Soul. She did not wish to converse with the entities any longer but she felt they would stay, lingering on about her until...

She knew the answer came from Soul. The voice or high-pitched sounds were the only reliable interpreter. As the melody filtered through her being they gave answer.

The answer was simple.

The entities would stay, linger on about her until she recognized them. Long ago, she had learned that recognition of illusion had the power to immediately dispel it. She would learn who the entities were.

"Do you have names?" Deetra called out to them.

"Oh yes, we have names," the one called back.

"It would be easier to speak to you if I knew them," Deetra said.

The one stared at her suspiciously. It seemed to sense her uneasiness more than the others. "If I tell you, will you join us?" the one asked.

"I don't know," she said.

"Then I can't tell you," the one said.

Deetra knew that she could not give her word to join them and then not do it. She was Askan and it was impossible to bargain and not uphold the agreement made. If she did so, she would fall into the clutches of the negative force. And if she agreed and kept her agreement she might still fall into the hands of the negative force. It might be the negative force asking her to join it.

"I can make no such agreement," she said to them.

"Then neither can we," the one said. "Neither can we."

Deetra shifted her attention to her husband Ian. He was the Hanta, the all powerful one, the Godman. Why was he not at her side, guiding her? Why had Malitara Tatz left her to be confronted by such absurd entities? She knew the answer of course. The Hanta was always with her in spirit. She need only ask for guidance and it would be received. But she had not done it for a long time, not since her marriage to Ian. Since then she had felt it was her responsibility to strengthen her own spiritual legs; to learn to stand alone so to speak, but perhaps she was carrying it too far. Perhaps she was forgetting that the Hanta was a permanent resident at the private temple within herself. She could no more eliminate the Hanta from her being any more than she could eliminate the sound of the Divine Force. They were One, Unlimited!

She caught herself on the thought.

It was true.

[*106*]

They were the One, Unlimited!

Why then was she insistent on limiting them?

Answers which had plagued her since her husband's departure now came pouring in on her. *She had been trying to limit the limitless power.* She had been guiding the village students to the Hanta, while feeling that she herself was apart from the advice. Did she feel herself so capable of standing alone that she did not need the Hanta?

Her thoughts ambled about the question, recalling how at the beginning of this journey she had come to realize that she had become comfortable in her spiritual position, wishing to remain where she was, believing that nothing could truly be beyond it. She had become master of herself on the level she had attained, but the level was limited, even though inwardly she contested that she could not see the limits. The very fact that she was comfortable and resisted following Malitara Tatz to the summit of Hanta's presence proved that point.

But what of the entities which awaited her instead of Hanta?

She looked up to the faces peering down at her from the summit. They were not smiling now. They were looking at her with some sadness in their faces, as though they were an inward witness to her turmoil.

Were they?

No. The impression was firm. The peering faces could not see into her. They were entities of a lower nature. Yet they seemed to know what it was she was exploring within herself. Also their expressions seemed to change as she met the changes within herself. She first noticed it when a wave of remorse washed through her. She was looking up at them when the feeling came and she thought of how secure and pompous she had felt telling the village students of what she knew to be truth. The beings watching her suddenly took on an expression which perfectly matched her feeling.

But how?

They were not of higher consciousness, nor were they equal to herself.

Or were they?

It was as though a clap of thunder sounded within her and instantly she knew. Looking up at the entities watching her, she realized that they were not outside of herself but a part of it. They were her physical senses. The one with large eyes was her eyes, the large nose her powers of scent, the ears her hearing, large mouth her speech and her taste, and the one who was the speaker of all was her feelings. They were aspects of her and being so were also aspects of her consciousness. They had become accustomed to certain things and certain ways and they were bound by the habits her consciousness formed. In a sense they were part of the consciousness.

That was why she was now confronted by them.

Suddenly she understood.

The entities of her senses had come forward as she was approaching the summit. Already she had realized that she had grown comfortable within herself. Now she was to see the meaning of that comfort. She was to confront her senses and see for herself the lackadaisical habit patterns they had assumed. It was what they had been trying to tell her; that she would have to meet with them before entering the land of Nome. Strange that they should know. Were they so connected to her consciousness that they had assumed intelligence of it?

Yes.

Deetra looked up at the peering faces and she felt deep compassion. She had imprisoned their expression, created their habits, made them slaves to pleasure, to likes and dislikes and, in so doing, she had molded their forms into the forms they had become. They had become visible entities—to herself, and surely to other Askan. Was that what the old messenger had tried to convey through his presence? She thought of Malitara Tatz and how he approached her

[*108*]

with stern affection, always prodding her not to remain still.

That was it.

Memories of the old messenger crept toward her with great clarity. He was always present when she had withdrawn into herself, as if prodding her into the village marketplace where she had encountered a part of her nature; into the Village Square working with other students. Malitara Tatz had gone to great lengths to show her without telling her, mocking up experiences and thought forms to break up those rigid ones she had built herself. He had even taken her to Liether the bodyless one and now he literally led her to the summit to meet with the Godman and to enter the land of Nome. Only first, it was necessary for her to meet herself and to dissolve the entities of herself. There was no other way.

But how?

There was no mystery to the question. The answer was simple. She had recognized the entities and recognition was all it took to dispel them. Quietly she sat down on the rock and looked up at her creations. "I bless you in the name of the Hanta," she said softly. Then she closed her eyes and began to sing the magical song of HU. When next she opened her eyes, the entities on the ledge above her had disappeared.

Malitara Tatz was standing next to her. She gazed at the spiritual adept and rose to her feet, smiling triumphantly.

"Ah, I see you have conquered the little self," the adept said, gazing back at her.

"For the moment," she said, "yet I am sure there is more to come."

"There is always more," Malitara Tatz said, "and with each step on the path the challenge of the little self becomes more subtle. Sometimes it is very difficult to recognize the little self. The ego has many disguises and it slips forward in our daily life without the slightest warning."

Deetra studied the kindly features of the adept's face.

His face was firm and bold and yet his eyes were gentle and filled with love. Could it be that one so close to SUG-MAD could still be affected by the little self?

The adept smiled as though he had heard her question but did not answer. "It is time we ascend the summit," he said lightly. "It is time you enter the land of Nome."

CHAPTER 11

When they had ascended the summit Deetra stood quite still, catching her breath more from what she saw than from the climb. All about were clear white domes. The ground about and near them was covered with green grasses and pink clovers, dotted by tiny white flowers that seemed to reach out and catch the sun's rays. Near the domes were delicately formed trees with leafy branches which canopied the landscape and they were covered with jewel-like fruits, reflecting red and gold as they glistened in the sunlight. She turned to Malitara Tatz, but he was not there.

She scanned the landscape, looking for him and then her attention was drawn to the sounds of a strange, alluring music unlike any she had heard. The melody was both high and low, intermittent with long spaces of silence between each note. It drew her attention and held it there as though she was reaching out to grasp each sound before it came to her and, as she listened in this intense way, she also heard the sounds of distant voices, but only gradually did she become aware of them.

Looking about at the dome-shaped structures, Deetra became aware that there were sounds of life coming from within them. The sounds seemed muffled, distorted by the enclosures and yet there was no doubt that they were distinctly human. Again she scanned the area for Malitara Tatz but he was not to be seen. Could it be that she was hearing his voice?

She walked to the dome nearest her and slowly walked around the structure, studying it. It was pure white and yet clear as though transparent, yet she could not see through it. There was no door of any kind nor were there any windows. It appeared improbable that anyone or anything was residing within and yet her experiences with the divine light and sound of SUGMAD often proved the improbable to be probable.

Turning, she went to the other domes, nine in all, and she walked around them as well and, seeing that they were all the same, she fell back, again listening to the powerful music of the spheres.

Malitara Tatz had left her, she knew, because the experience before her demanded solitary recognition.

But of what?

The domes were spread out in a circle. Deetra sat down in the center of them and waited. It was here she had supposed that she would meet Ian and those who had joined him. Malitara Tatz had left her below the summit to confront the hidden aspects of herself and had reappeared when the task was complete. He had then led her to this place only to once again leave her to discover something.

But what?

What was expected of her?

Was she to meet still another part of herself; to recognize the solitary confinement of Soul in yet another way?

As she asked the question a great rush of wind came toward her and she quickly rose to her feet. Then the wind stopped and everything fell into absolute stillness. There was nothing. Even the haunting music of the spheres seemed to obey the call for silence.

She was without thought.

The silence enveloped her.

After what seemed a long moment her mind pushed forward, questioning her whereabouts and, as it did, the sounds of the environment—the wind and the voices—

seemed to rush back at her. Gradually, when she quieted her mind once again, it all stopped.

So that was it!

The realization crept toward her like a thief in the night. At first she couldn't grasp it. It alluded her until the mind was drawn forth in an odd state of balance. It was not active nor inactive, not questioning or analyzing, nor still. Gradually it came into a state of being that was neither questioning nor answering, neither for nor against anything. It was balanced between the poles of being and non-being and in this state or condition, she became aware of a subtle beingness that she had never before realized. She was the cause and the effect of everything.

She was the *it* and the *non-it*.

What she saw and experienced was how she was seeing things; how she perceived them; her viewpoint shifting about the environment.

She stood still, lost in thought. Suddenly, she saw her whole life flash before her and she also saw herself viewing the circumstances of her life. It was her attitude toward each incident that created her vision of it, and her vision became her point of view.

The most painful experience in her life was when, as a child, her mother died, yet it was an extraordinary experience and one she would never forget. At first she believed her mother to be deserting her and she was angry, and then the anger yielded to fear and loneliness, and finally the fear and loneliness, yielded to acceptance and understanding. The shifting in her viewpoints toward this experience came about in an evolutionary way via changes in her attitudes about what death was. As she had accepted her new understandings, she acknowledged a change in attitude and accepted a different view of her circumstances. Thus she shifted her point of view, until finally, she reached a comfortable circumstance, one which she could live happily and progressively within.

Deetra also recalled her feelings when she learned that Ian, then her husband to be, had accepted the rod of power and had become Hanta. There was no doubt in her mind that she had loved Ian as a spiritual being as well as a man, but to marry a man who was the Hanta, the Godman, was not a circumstance to be taken lightly. As much as she loved the man and the spiritual path, she had to retreat within herself to adjust the attitudes which she had in the past held about the Hanta so that her point of view could adjust to meet the circumstances. There was no way that she could honestly concede to marrying, without true spiritual realization of what the Hanta title meant. To do so would have created catastrophe and total self-destruction. And too, she had to accept the responsibility of merging with the man who bore the spiritual power.

Deetra remembered how she had considered life without Ian; how in imagination she had lived without him only to realize the emptiness of that life. She thought of him now as well. Since his departure she had moved ahead in her own spiritual development. It had been difficult at times and usually the difficulty had been in those long moments between time and space when she had hesitated, not wishing to take the next step. And then there had been those times when she did not know how to take the next step or where it was. Often Malitara Tatz had tried to guide her; to encourage her in a direction and still she did not catch on. It had been a long, difficult road since her husband had left on his journey, and yet it had been an exciting one.

It was not over yet.

Malitara Tatz, she knew, had brought her here and left her for a purpose. She knew she would not meet with Ian until that purpose was fulfilled.

Deetra looked about at the domes encircling her. She counted them once again. Nine. Nine in all, and all nine appeared to be exactly the same. There was the difference in location in that one was located to the front of her at a particular angle and another at another angle, and some to the side at still other angles, and yet as she turned to face each, the angle adjusted itself. It was relative, she thought, all a matter of how she viewed each within the whole.

That was it.

The role of viewpoint applied in some mystical way. But what did it mean?

Was the mystery of the domes locked in her vision of them?

If she saw them differently, would her circumstances on the summit be different?

She thought of Malitara Tatz and wondered if, although he was unseen, he was present on the summit. If she viewed the environment from a different point of reference would she be aware of him and others not presently visible?

The idea held her attention as she moved slowly in and around the dome-shaped structures. No sounds came from within and in the stillness she listened for the sound current of SUGMAD.

At first she heard nothing. It was as though the stillness was amplified but, gradually, she became aware of a subtle sound, a soft hum that radiated through the silence. She tried to distinguish it from the stillness itself but could not. *It was the stillness, the voice of it* and then she realized that the stillness was the current of SUGMAD. It was the voice of *it*.

Then it struck her.

The domes were the stillness from which the current of SUGMAD came.

The domes were a manifestation of SUGMAD.

In the realization her senses rose in excitement and then calmed again. She focused her attention on that point between the eyebrows called the tisra til or spiritual eye and quickly succeeded in balancing mind. Then she allowed the realization to rise in her again.

If the domes were a manifestation of SUGMAD, then

she, too, was a manifestation of SUGMAD. She had realized this long ago on her arrival to the City of Light where she had met the true nature of herself—Soul— and recognized her beingness as that. Yet the realization was never complete until now. *Now she saw Soul as SUGMAD.*

The domes blurred in her vision, seemingly connected by links of herself and spun about her. She was encircled by them, encircled by herself; sheafs of matter forming layers about her true reality—the reality of all. And the circle began to spin, building up momentum to the point where she was no longer in the center of the circle but a part of it. She and the domes were blended into one.

Suddenly it stopped.

The stillness hummed back at her as she stood in the center of the circle of domes. Then she saw that the domes were not solid but particles of light joined together to appear solid and she herself was the same.

She held out her hand before her. An extension of light followed from the eggshaped wholeness of her form. As her gaze followed the extension, her attention lighted on the domes about her. They were as she was—not domes at all. They were form in light and now, for the first time, she saw what they were.

They were people.

At first she could not make out their identities, just that they were people, and then as she adjusted her senses to accept what it was she was seeing, she saw who it was.

Ian!

Malitara Tatz!

Ramus-i-Rabriz!

And there were others who seemed familiar although she did not know them by name.

"Welcome my beloved," Ian said, outstretching a hand to her. "Welcome to the land of Nome."

Too astonished to speak, Deetra moved to him and took his outstretched hand and, as she did, the warmth of his love passed from him and filled her. She smiled at him warmly.

"And those who join me," Ian asked. "do you recognize them?"

Deetra turned to the circle of figures, her eyes alighting on Ramus-i-Rabriz and she bowed slightly. It seemed a long time since she had been with the temple master and she recalled how he had introduced her to the doorways between the worlds and the chamber of tests where her initiation had taken place. She smiled at him warmly.

Ramus-i-Rabriz looked upon her kindly but did not speak.

Then she turned to Malitara Tatz and nodded a greeting. It seemed the adept always appeared in her life at the high moments. He winked at her but did not smile.

Deetra shifted her gaze to the others. One was a tall, lean, bald man wearing little more than a loin cloth. She had seen him before somewhere, although she had no conscious memory of him until now. And the man next to him was also familiar. The long white beard and piercing eyes held her gaze for a moment, then she looked to the next and to the next.

Suddenly she hesitated.

Before her was not a man but a woman and the only one present other than herself. She could not help but stare at her strangely. With careful eyes she saw that this woman was unlike any woman she had known. Her appearance was matronly and yet she carried herself in such a way that she appeared to be a woman of great position and beauty. She had a gentle face, piercing blue eyes and dark hair turned under at the nape of her neck, and she wore a casual white gown with gold threads woven through it. She smiled at Deetra and extended her hand to her.

"My name is Kara," she said kindly, "and I am pleased to meet Deetra the wife of Ian, though I have seen you many times before now."

As though caught in a vision, Deetra reached out and took Kara's outstretched hand and, as she did, she was aware that her other hand still rested in Ian's and that the warm flow of her husband's love was passing through her to Kara and returning. The meeting was a union and for a split second the three with clasped hands silently were wrapped in a globe of light, the songs of SUGMAD passing through them and the others were with them, *one* with them, and the three too were *one*. And then, just as suddenly, the vision dissolved and Deetra stood alone on the summit or so she thought.

Kara was still there.

The others, including Ian, had vanished.

Kara wore a kindly but sober expression, waiting for Deetra's attention.

"I have remained to explore Nome with you," Kara said, "but I see that first there is something you wish to ask me."

Deetra did not try to hide her feelings from this woman adept. She knew there was no point to it; that the adept knew all that she thought and felt. She wanted to know why, although she understood the positive and negative energies, she had seen no other women in the high spiritual ranks, and what Kara had achieved to be there? Deetra thought these things but did not say them aloud.

"There are many of us," Kara said. "The female is no less a spiritual being than the male. Actually it is the recognition that we are both the male and the female within ourselves that raises us to the heights of realization—the male being positive and the female being the negative polarity. When we realize the dual nature within ourselves we are no longer limited by our outward gender. I am woman, but most of all, I am a composite of the two genders, which means I am a spiritual being."

Kara paused, looking deeply into Deetra before continuing: "Marriage is a spiritual exercise," she said, "It provides the contract for a merger between the two forces. It is not the only way and therefore not a necessity, but it is the most practical and efficient way. Marriage means union and once the spiritual recognition of it takes place, the physical becomes a joyful state of companionship for the two people involved."

Deetra thought of Ian and their marriage. It was indeed a spiritual exercise filled with inner discoveries. It was a union of constant inner motion, without rest. It was the height of all life and yet she was outside it as well as within it. Being married to the man who bore the power of Hanta could not be the same, she knew, as being married to an ordinary man.

"It is both the same and not the same," Kara said, answering her thought. "There is a side of Ian that is an ordinary man and that makes your union the same as any other. And there is Ian, the spiritual man, advanced beyond the ordinary, who carries the mantle of power. Your marriage with him is quite different than an ordinary marriage but then the advantages are quite extraordinary." Kara looked deeply into Deetra. "And you are a spiritual woman, advanced beyond the ordinary or else you would not have attracted such power," Kara said.

Deetra looked at the woman warmly. "Thank you," she said. "I suppose you remained when the others left to tell me that."

"That and other things," Kara said, smiling. "You are now ready to explore Nome."

Kara moved silently ahead of Deetra, leading her to the very height of the summit, a rise in the middle of a ring of spruce trees. There was a stream running through it, and it was there that she pointed to a rock next to the fast-moving water where she asked Deetra to sit down.

"Nome is not an outward experience but rather an inward one which sees outward," Kara said, watching as Deetra took her seat on the rock next to the stream. She did not speak again until Deetra had settled herself. "Would you repeat what I have just said to you," Kara asked.

Deetra looked at the woman seated next to her, her knees drawn up to her chin. She appeared younger than when they first met. "You said, *Nome is not an outward experience but rather an inward one which sees outward,*" Deetra repeated.

"Good," Kara said, "I see you were listening after all." She smiled. "Now that you have absorbed that statement, I would like to alter it. We have just called *Nome an experience. It is that but it is more than that. It is what we see through the face of God.*" She paused, studying Deetra, then continued: "Not long ago, you discovered Nome to be consciousness, did you not?"

"Yes."

"And that is correct. Nome is your consciousness, my dear, not someone else's, although you may meet someone else's within your own." She hesitated. "Do I make myself clear?"

Deetra looked into the deep-set blue eyes and saw what she had seen in Malitara Tatz's eyes—a tiny image of herself. She was caught by it, witnessing herself within another. Was that what Kara meant?

"You understand and yet not completely," Kara said. "Return to that understanding and reach into it even deeper."

Deetra shifted her gaze about the adept's face. She suddenly appeared very old and when she again looked into the image of herself within Kara's eyes, she saw that she too had aged.

What did it mean?

As quickly as the question formed in her, it vanished. Within the tiny image of herself, she saw other images. There was Tolar and the physician Sonar and other villagers, as well as the adepts she had met here on the summit. She saw the old messenger translated into the image of Malitara Tatz and with him she saw the invalid Liether.

Liether called to her, beckoning with an invisible arm. Deetra stared at the image of the man. He could not move his body, not any part of it. The man was completely paralyzed yet there was the presence of his arm waving for her to come near.

She watched him, then realized that the image of the paralyzed man was not merely a vision passing through Kara's eyes. As she moved closer to Liether, she could see that he was real and whole. His lifeless body had a life to it, and the life was independent of his body.

"Deetra," he called, motioning her to him. "Do you see what I've learned? Isn't it wonderful Deetra!"

Deetra studied the man. Particles of light gathered about him and formed a brilliant spectacle. The lifeless arm did not move, but the one made of light did and so did the legs, which were made of light. They moved and ran toward her while the lifeless body remained behind.

"Do you remember what the old messenger asked me?" Liether asked.

Deetra did not answer but shook her head.

"Remember the clay pot on the fireplace shelf?" Liether asked. "Remember how it was identified as the pot which held the flint, and the old messenger asked me if I thought the flint was confined to the pot?"

"Yes," Deetra answered absently, drawing the event to memory. "I remember."

"Well, I said that it was confined until someone re-moved it," Liether said. "You do remember that?"

"Yes."

"Well then, that's the point," Liether said.

"What is?" Deetra asked, aware of the activity of his *light* body. It moved agitatedly about her.

"The old messenger asked me another question. He wanted me to tell him if the pot had an identity with the flint after the flint was removed," Liether said impatiently.

Deetra did not answer.

"Can't you see?"

"I see that you have discovered the secret for your freedom," Deetra said.

"But that's just it!" Liether said.

"What is?"

"The answer for what I have now realized," Liether said.

"I don't understand," Deetra said, shaking her head.

"Of course you do. You've just forgotten," Liether said. "I answered the old messenger's question by saying that 'one was the vessel for the other.' Do you remember it now?"

"Vaguely," Deetra said thoughtfully, "but I can see that you do."

"You can bet I do. Look at me," Liether said. "I'm whole! Just look at me!"

It was true, Liether was whole, not physically, and yet he was no longer hampered by his physical body. He could venture from it freely. Suddenly it dawned on Deetra that he had discovered the relationship of his *light* body with his physical body. The *light* body was invisible to most, and yet as a vehicle, it provided total freedom for Liether.

"You still don't understand, do you?" Liether said sadly.

"I think I do," Deetra said, "and I'm happy for you Liether."

"Happy for me," Liether said hesitantly, "you should be happy for yourself. Can't you see what has happened?"

Deetra was puzzled and did not answer.

Liether shook his head. "You are the one who gave me the answer," he said.

"But how?" she said, "I don't remember it. And what does it matter anyway. You have your answers. Anyone can see that you have achieved the answers."

"But so have you!" Liether shouted.

Deetra studied the intense expression on the man's

[*122*]

face. He was obviously frustrated that she did not truly hear what he was saying. "I'm sorry," she said finally. "I don't seem to understand what you are trying to tell me."

"I'm in Nome!" Liether said loudly, reaching a hand from his radiant body and touching her. "I'm in Nome and so are you."

It was true, Deetra was in Nome, although for a time she had forgotten it. She had been sitting, looking into Kara's eyes and had become fascinated with a tiny image of herself which she saw there. But it was not only herself who she saw. She had seen many, and she was visiting with Liether. Liether was in Nome. He said so. He was aware of being in Nome. How incredible! And even more incredible was her own awareness of being in Nome. She was in Nome with Liether but she was also in Nome with the adept Kara. Then she remembered how she had looked into Kara's eyes and gone beyond the image of herself to find the others.

She looked away, suddenly aware of Kara's presence once again; aware that the adept was looking at her and gradually she raised her eyes to meet hers.

"What did you see?" Kara asked.

Deetra shook her head.

"You know," Kara said. "It is important now that you tell me."

Deetra told the adept about Liether; how he had appeared and about their communication.

"Is that all?" Kara asked. "Did you see no one else?"

"Yes," Deetra said nodding. "I saw others from the village."

"Did they recognize you?" Kara prodded.

"No, they did not seem to be aware of me," Deetra said.

Kara studied the girl patiently. "If Liether was in Nome where do you suppose the others where when you saw them?" Kara asked.

"I don't know."

"Yes, you do."

Deetra looked into the kindly face. She wanted to say again that she did not know, but she knew that she could not allow herself to say it. She was an Askan on the summit in Nome, a place of high consciousness. She could no longer permit herself ignorance. "They were in Nome as well," she said finally.

Kara smiled. "That is correct, dear one," she said, "but tell me, are they in Nome now?"

Deetra looked about, uncertain. Again she wanted to plead that she did not know, but she knew that she could not do it. She must not. "Malitara Tatz is in Nome," she said hesitantly.

"And who else?" Kara prodded.

"Liether," Deetra said.

Kara smiled again. "Yes, he most certainly is," she said, "and he seems to be enjoying his adventures. But what about the others?"

Kara had seen Deetra's vision.

"Say what you know, dear one," Kara prodded.

"They are not in Nome," Deetra said. "I saw them. They were in Nome when I saw them but they are not now."

"And why is that, dear one?"

Deetra shook her head and turned away.

"You know the answer, dear one," Kara said again. "Admit to yourself that you know and say it aloud."

Deetra drew in a deep breath and looked into the kindly face. "They were in Nome," she said slowly, "because I was when I saw them. My thoughts drew them."

Kara nodded thoughtfully. "That is true," she said patiently, "but there is more."

Deetra looked into Kara's eyes and again saw the tiny image of herself. She moved into the image and through it, thinking of Tolar and of the physician, seeing them instantly as her imagination formed them. There seemed to be nothing of interest about their situation. She saw the two of

[*124*]

them conversing and she would have listened except that she knew that what they were saying would explain nothing to her. She was not interested in the mundane matters of conversation. She was interested in finding out their circumstances in Nome.

But how?

They did not have the consciousness to be in Nome.

Or did they?

Just then a number of the other villagers passed by the physician and Tolar. They nodded in greeting and went about their conversation.

Were the other villagers in Nome also?

She did not draw their presence to her. She had drawn Tolar and Sonar, but no one else.

Gradually, watching the scene, she became aware of a subtle realization stalking her. Patiently, she waited for it to unfold.

It seemed that while she was aware of them, they were not aware of her, meaning to Deetra that they were in Nome but did not know that they were. She saw them. She knew they were in Nome but they didn't, except Liether. Liether had discovered Nome's existence within himself as she had and his discovery had empowered him with its freedom.

That was it!

Everyone had to discover Nome for themselves. Then it hit her all at once. *Everyone was in Nome. All the villagers were there; all the villagers from every village. All beings were there.*

There?

No, *here. Nome was here in the now of every being. It WAS, IS and WILL BE. Nome was the consciousness of ALL and of each unit or being of the ALL. But for all that it was, Nome was nothing until it was recognized by the individual consciousness within it, except that without Nome there could be no consciousness, no life, no beingness. Nome was everything.*

All beings—man and animal were in Nome, only it was rare indeed to find one who was aware of it.

Yes, that was it!

It was the awareness of Nome that was its value. If one did not know where he was, Nome was of no avail. It could benefit him not at all except . . . Deetra stopped, catching herself in the conclusion. It was not true that it could not benefit without awareness.

Nome was a force which sustained life.

But it was more than that; more than the force.

Nome was the force behind the force. It was the beingness—which made existence possible and, moreover, Nome was the presenter, the image, presented by the imager. It was the face, so to speak, of all living things.

Nome was the face of God.

The awareness struck Deetra with tremendous force, jolting her physically, shocking her as though she had touched upon the veil of SUGMAD, peeked at the Deity only to quickly back away.

Kara was sitting opposite her along the stream, watching her. "And now you see, dear one," she said excitedly, "and now you see."

Deetra sat upright, looking into the face of the kindly adept. A surge of love rose in her and went out to Kara, thanking her with divine feeling. She wanted to speak the words of gratitude but could not. She was speechless, struck dumb.

Kara nodded at Deetra with understanding. Then she drew her knees up to her chin and smiled warmly. "You have it now," she said warmly. "Dear one, you have it now!"

CHAPTER 12

Being in Nome, so Deetra discovered, was no different than being anywhere else in that there were feelings and use of the other senses just as there was in the physical world, except that in Nome, one had to use these senses to propel the self into different areas of consciousness. In the worlds of matter, the senses worked automatically and, on the contrary, steered the individual into like experiences. To be aware of Nome one had to be in control.

Kara first brought this fact forward when she suggested that Deetra practice the art of doing without doing; that is, to be still while using the imagination to draw the experience to her.

"Imagination is Soul's thought, so to speak," Kara explained. "When we allow imagination to be positively creative then we are utilizing the powers of Nome." Then she left Deetra sitting on the rock next to the stream to discover for herself the truth in what she had just said.

At first Deetra was timid about the method to proceed. She imagined little things like moving about the summit and the things that she saw there. Then she became more bold. She remembered how she had spoken with Liether and how, although when she had seen Tolar and the physician conversing, she had accepted the fact that she could not communicate with them because they knew nothing of Nome. Suppose she had tried to tell them of it. She decided to test the idea.

Using her imagination she propelled herself to the Village Square as though she expected there to be a class, and sat waiting for those interested to show up. After a brief period a few of the students ambled into the square and sat down. Tolar and the physician Sonar were among them. At first they sat absently staring at one another, wondering if there was to be class and then a calm, patient silence came among them. They appeared to be meditating.

In invisible presence, Deetra started class. First she sang the HU, after which she began to tell them of Nome, of the dwelling place within themselves, and explained that their awareness of its existence was what made true reality. When she was finished, she walked around the square, gently touching each student. "May the blessings Be!" she said to each, pausing to grasp the significance, if any, of their meeting.

There were no outward appearances recognizing her but many held thoughts of her image as though they were seeing her inwardly. She could not tell if any had truly heard her.

She moved out of the square and stood looking at them. Some were beginning to talk among themselves, while some seemed to look in the direction she had gone as though they expected to see her there. "Suppose," said one, "Deetra was here and we couldn't see her." The attention of those nearby turned to the one who had spoken. It was as if they accepted the statement as possibility. Then they began to talk among themselves on the subject of unseen existence.

Deetra opened her eyes expecting Kara to be there but she was alone. She thought of what had transpired a moment before in the Village Square, and she felt with some satisfaction that she had been successful in communicating Nome to her students. It may be that they haven't consciously grasped the name of Nome, but they seemed to be becoming aware of some of its aspects. For them, it was a beginning.

Deetra hesitated a moment, thinking about the conclusion she had just made. Her students seemed to be so quick, so ripe for discovery, whereas it seemed that it had taken her longer to reach the point where they were now. Could it be that they were more advanced Souls; that they were more ready for the next step than she when she began?

It seemed likely. Most of her students had received crystals long ago, even though they only now began to use them. She herself had received her crystal one day and began use of it immediately. When she was ready for it, she received it and used it, whereas it seemed they had waited a very long time, nearly a lifetime for some, to use their crystals. No wonder they moved so rapidly, awakening swiftly. They were past the point of being ready.

Then Deetra thought of Liether. Her meeting with him had seemed incomplete, as though she had missed the point of their meeting in some way. She imagined him coming toward her. She saw the man in detail, in the radiant body, and she called out to him on the inner planes, asking to speak with him.

Liether stood before her smiling. "What is it, my friend?" he asked.

"Would you tell me what you have discovered of Nome?" she asked.

Liether's expression grew serious and thoughtful. He did not answer for a moment, then said, "Freedom. That's what I've learned. I've found that as long as my mind does not double back upon me with doubts and questions, I can live in a lifeless body and be free of it at the same time. And in my freedom, I am whole and mobile. There is nothing I cannot do or learn. You said yourself that everything I have experienced you have experienced as well."

"I did?" Deetra asked with some surprise.

"Yes, when you visited me at my mother's with the old messenger," Liether said. "You told me that you went through the tribulations of gaining freedom and that it was part of the trials of becoming Askan." Liether searched Deetra's face. "Don't you remember?" he asked.

Deetra hesitated, unsure.

"You are Askan?" Liether asked.

Deetra looked at the man and nodded. "Yes, of course," she said softly.

"Well, I'm not yet," Liether said, looking deeply at her.

Deetra felt humbled by the man's gaze. Why should she be Askan when he had known of Nome before she had?

The answer came quickly, rushing toward her as she questioned her right to be Askan. She had earned the title before learning of Nome; before that time and differently. She had journeyed Moonwalk; had met the negative forces head on and had effected a merger with the Hanta consciousness to reach the City of Light. She had no reason to feel humbled in the presence of this man.

"You will become Askan in the right time," she said sincerely. "Meanwhile you are enjoying the splendors of Nome." She smiled, pausing. "It seems a fine lot."

Liether nodded uncomfortably. "I suppose," he said, "yet sometimes, I am disturbed because I feel I have earned the right and have been cheated."

Deetra did not try to relate to the feeling, remembering and heeding Malitara Tatz's warning not to become prey to another's feelings. "Things are not always as they appear," Deetra said.

"What do you mean?" Liether asked.

"The mind sometimes has a way of twisting reality," Deetra said. "Sometimes when feelings of desire reach out to us, the mind becomes empowered to act upon the feeling, and things seem to us not as they really are."

"Meaning I am not yet fit to be Askan," Liether said strongly.

"You are fit," Deetra said, "or else you would not be shown the glories of Nome."

[*130*]

"Then what do you mean?"

"That your time will come," Deetra said.

"Is that all?" Liether asked.

"I cannot speak for the Hanta," Deetra said.

Liether looked at her with hard expression. "Do you mean to tell me that the Hanta chooses who will be Askan?" he asked.

"Yes."

"That no one else, meaning another Askan does not recommend another to be Askan," Liether said, annoyed.

"If that were to be true it would make no difference," Deetra said.

"I don't understand!"

"When spiritually you become Askan, you become Askan," Deetra said. "There is no plainer way to say it."

"There are higher forces at work then," Liether said.

"Absolutely."

"I wish it to be true," Liether said thoughtfully.

"It is true."

"What would you suggest I do to improve myself?" Liether asked eagerly.

Deetra did not answer right away but waited for the soft hum of HU to sound in her inner ear. "Use your advantage to roam Nome to find your answer," Deetra suggested.

"In what way?"

"Hold your inner vision on the Hanta," Deetra said. "It is the way of the Askan. From there you can learn everything there is to learn."

"You mean it?" Liether asked.

"I mean it," Deetra said, smiling. Then she thanked him for sharing his discovery of Nome and bid him farewell. "We will visit many times," she said, "but for now, I have work to do."

Liether looked at her questioningly but did not ask. "See you soon," he said warmly, "and thank you." Then he left.

[*131*]

Kara looked at Deetra and shook her head from side to side. "You think you've done it all, don't you, dear one?" she asked.

Deetra did not know what to answer.

"Think now, dear one," Kara said. "Shut your eyes and think about what you have just experienced and tell me what you think comes next." Then she raised her hand, motioning Deetra to close her eyes.

Deetra was obedient but suddenly confused. She did not know what Kara expected of her and the adept's mind projected no clues.

Behind closed eyelids, Deetra watched the darkness turn into a soft white light. It became more and more brilliant as she looked at it with her inner eyes. As it became all encompassing, sound seemed to pop from it. It was the thin, high-pitched alluring sound of the force of life and, as it hummed its song through her, she thought of her husband, Ian, the Hanta. It was time, it seemed, that she called him to her and in that instant she did.

Ian was there, next to her, his hand resting upon hers, his eyes gazing not at her but into her. It was Ian, the Hanta, who was looking at her, but there was also a certain tenderness projecting which told her that it was also Ian, the man, her husband.

"I have missed you greatly, dearest," Ian said softly.

"And I have missed you," Deetra answered.

Then in that moment they were together, closely together, lying on the ground next to the stream, embracing. It was a moment of total rapture, a merging together of being within being, the light and sounds of HU penetrating their togetherness, uniting them into a single complete being. They were the light, the brilliant white light and they were the song of their own togetherness. They were one with *it* and they were themselves one with one another. There was a secret, silent part of herself which Deetra was merging with her husband and in the merger she was not sure where she began and her husband ended. They were truly two forces—two polarities joined together creating a single unit.

Then it struck her!

Here in Nome they had become *one!* She was the negative polarity, the female, and Ian the positive, the male, and yet now they were both BOTH. She had become the positive as well, and he had become the negative as well. They had united and merged their powers into a single unit.

"It is a moment I have awaited," Ian said softly.

Deetra lifted her head and looked into her lover's eyes. She did not even know until now that such a union existed, although inwardly she had yearned for a part of herself as yet unfulfilled. Was it true that in the union she had connected herself to the power her husband wielded?

"Yes," Ian said softly, his cheek next to hers. "And from you I gain the completeness of Soul as well."

Deetra searched his eyes for an answer. "In what way?" she asked, suddenly uneasy.

"In every way," he answered.

"Tell me," she begged.

He held her tightly once again and closed his eyes. She closed hers as well and in the faint glow of her inner vision she saw into her husband's heart. Within him was herself and with herself came an opposite power than his own. It balanced him as he balanced her, but differently. He was the light and the power. She, on the other hand, was the perceiver of that light and power, of all it could accomplish. She was the intuitive self, the knowing self and the feeling self which ignited and directed the masculine or positive power.

Still Deetra had to know more.

Within her union she separated herself from Ian and saw him alone, without her, the positive force only. He was only half whole without her. There was no emotional depth without her and his vision and understanding were limited by his isolation. Deetra, on the other hand, had all the feeling and the vision and understanding, but she lacked the power to give them effectiveness. Seeing this, she re-entered Ian's heart and became one with him again.

"And that's how it is, beloved," Ian said gently. "To be united is to be whole, *one* with self and one with *all.*"

Deetra sat up and touched the ground with her hands, shifting her fingers back and forth in the deep, rich soil. She looked away from Ian thoughtfully.

Ian did not speak but sat quietly, watching her.

Questions pounded at Deetra's thoughts. Kara had said that marriage was a spiritual exercise and that when true spiritual union took place within the individual, the individual became a balance of both polarities, not with another person, but within oneself. Why then was Ian only half without her? He was the Hanta!

Then her mind seized on Kara's last words *"Think now, dear one,"* she had said, *"think about what you have just experienced and tell me what you believe comes next."*

How odd!

Deetra had neglected thinking about Liether and her meeting with him and immediately looked toward the next moment, drawing Ian to her. Why had she done that? Kara had asked her to think of the experience just passed before drawing in the next. Why had she not done so?

"It does not matter," Ian said softly.

But it did and Deetra did not know why.

"Think then about Liether," Ian said again. "Let your experience with him expound itself and be done with it."

There was an abruptness in Ian's voice that caught Deetra by surprise, but she did not face him. She thought instead of Liether and the meaning of her conversation with him.

Liether had been troubled by the fact that he had the knowledge of an Askan but was not an Askan. He had felt cheated. Was that why he had been drawn to her in the first place?

She recalled her feeling when Liether first intimidated her for being Askan and he not, and she recalled how she had dismissed the feeling as well. He had challenged her as he would have challenged any Askan. It had nothing to do with her personally. It was simply that she was a symbol of all Askan, of a consciousness, a oneness with all, and for that reason he reached out to her as a part of himself.

The understanding came quietly, but it grew in her. It was as Ian had said. She was *one* with self as she was *one* with all. She did not need Ian any more than he needed her, but together they were a spiritual exercise of a union that was maintained in them.

Ian lightly touched her arm. "I love you, beloved," he said tenderly, "and in loving you, life is joyful. Can you accept me in my joy?"

Deetra slowly turned to face him. His eyes met hers eagerly. She smiled and touched her hand to his lips. "I accept you completely," she said sincerely.

"Then you accept the fact that I am Hanta as well," Ian said.

"Of course," she said, surprised that he had asked.

"Are you sure?"

"I don't understand you," she said, sitting up straight. "Why would I not accept the conciousness you possess?"

"Ahhh," said Ian, "then you accept your self within it as well."

Unsure, she did not answer.

"I mean to make it clear to you that if you are *one* with self and *one* with all, then you are *one* with the consciousness as well." Ian paused, studying the seriousness of Deetra's expression, and he smiled. "Beloved, do you know what I am saying?"

Deetra hesitated, slowly turning her head from side to side, watching as the smile disappeared from Ian's face.

"I am saying that you, beloved, because of our union

and bond, share the Hanta consciousness. You cannot be a step beneath me. You must be level to me in order to fill my heart with joy."

Deetra studied the sincere lines of her husband's face. There was nothing in his expression to betray what he had said, and she could feel nothing in his heart except love and confirmation. Did she then assume the Hanta consciousness?

"The key to higher consciousness," Ian said plainly, "is in the assumption of it. That is, you call on the higher consciousness, the Hanta consciousness, for guidance and then you assume its assistance. In that way, as you know, it comes to you bit by bit. The more you call on *it*, the more *it* responds. If you use *it* constantly, then *it* never fails you and so therefore after much dedication you assume *it,* becoming *it."* He took her hand and raised it to his lips. "In a way," he said softly, " you have always known this truth."

Deetra looked into her husband's eyes and knew that what he was saying was truth. She had always known it, and yet in many ways she had turned her back on this knowingness. It had frightened her. Suppose she were to be consumed by *it* and she knew that in yielding to *it* she would be consumed.

Ian rubbed her hand lightly and nodded in understanding. "You will find your time, my love," he said, "although I am waiting for you, I have no choice but to wait patiently. You need not rush nor worry about it. You will join me when you are ready."

A great feeling of separateness overwhelmed Deetra. It seemed there was suddenly visible between them a huge gulf and the distance was painful. Her heart ached, reaching out to him.

"Don't rush yourself, my love," Ian said, letting go of her hand. "It is not enough to reach out to me with feeling alone. When you are ready, I will still be waiting."

Deetra could not hold back the tears. They overflowed

her eyes and dripped down her cheeks. The pain she was feeling within was overwhelming her. She raised her hands to her face and wept lightly, then brushed the tears from her cheeks.

She turned to Ian but he was gone.

CHAPTER 13

For a long while Deetra sat alone next to the stream, thinking on what had transpired that afternoon. She thought of her class at the Village Square and how they had anticipated her presence, and of Liether, his certain, irrevocable belief in his freedom in Nome, and all the while an image of Ian hovered over her. She loved him. She loved him so much that she could barely tolerate herself for causing him to withdraw from her presence.

How could she have done so?

Occasionally a few tears would dribble down her face and she would brush them away. She knew that everything Ian had said to her was true. All she had to do was to allow herself to merge with the Hanta consciousness and *all* would be within her. She would be a total being.

Why then did a part of her refuse?

Was it not what she had always wanted?

Had she come this far only to deny herself the only accomplishment in life that had complete meaning?

She looked about hoping to see Kara or Malitara Tatz but she saw no one. Was she so completely deserted by those who once guided her?

She recalled how Malitara Tatz had previously walked off and left her. It had been her time of decision as to whether she would continue up the mountain or not. Was that why she was left alone now? To decide?

She knew that it was true. She had to decide for herself that she would take the next step, yet the decision, she knew, was greater than any other she had made. Before, the next step was only a step with hidden meaning, but now the next step was the final one it seemed. Beyond it, she had no more control. She would be a total instrument and, although it was the state of consciousness she had always dreamed of reaching, the height of all, she was terrified of it.

She did not want to be consumed.

She wanted to maintain her individuality; to be *one within one*. She wanted to give her all but, at the same time, she wanted to maintain a separateness.

What was it within her that denied the Hanta consciousness?

Restlessly, she rose from the rock next to the stream and stood absently looking about the summit. There were trails in every direction and as she hesitated, looking at them, she knew that her state of consciousness would pick the one she was to travel. She cautioned herself, then yielded to an impulse and set out on the path parallel to where she was.

She walked silently and slowly, not really wanting to stray far from the summit yet far enough to gain an overall perception of it, and as she went she thought of the other members of the Hanta's travelling party she had not seen on the summit. Her father, Starn, was among them and so was Rian, the scribe, or at least she believed they were. Starn had left from the Village Square to join the Hanta's pilgrimage. Had he somehow not found him?

It was doubtful. Starn was not a man to become easily misdirected. It was not likely that he had become lost in the mountains.

And what of Rian and the Chief Elder Sarpent? They had left with the Hanta, yet she had not met up with them.

Her thoughts went out to Starn. They had agreed to keep in close telepathic contact, yet she had become so engrossed in her own experiences she had completely forgotten her father? Had he been calling to her on the inner planes and she had not heard him?

It was as if her sudden rememberance was heard because a second later Starn was with her, holding her in a brief embrace. He whispered something to her that she did not understand. Then he held her at arms length and said it again.

"Daughter, you are in grave danger," Starn said, a look of concern etched on his face.

Deetra stared at him undisturbed. "In what way?" she asked.

"There are negative forces in Nome which have their roots elsewhere," Starn said.

"I don't understand you," Deetra said, searching her father's appearance for a clue. His clothes were slightly torn and rumpled. "Are you all right?" she asked.

Starn nodded. "I'm all right but there are others who are not," he said.

"What others?" she asked.

"Those in the Hanta's travelling party," Starn said. "Have you not met any of them?"

Deetra lowered her eyes momentarily and then raised them again. "I have seen the Hanta," she said, "and those adepts at his side. Are they who you mean?"

"No, the others!"

"What others?"

"Sarpent and Rian," Starn said, "and the others."

"Father, you are not speaking plainly," Deetra said. "Please say what it is that you know."

Starn drew in a deep breath and exhaled slowly. "When I met up with the Hanta's party, they had been separated from the Hanta and the other adepts. Many were suffering from fatigue and exposure. I tried to assist them in the best ways I could by attending to their wounds, but it did not help. And so I left them and came to seek assistance. That is when your thoughts drew me to you."

"Where are they now?" Deetra asked.

"They are scattered about the mountain. Last seen Sarpent and Rian were heading for Moonwalk to rescue the others." Starn paused, looking deeply into his daughter's eyes. "The others are those from the village," he said.

"But this is impossible," Deetra said.

"In what way?"

"Moonwalk does not exist in Nome," Deetra said.

"It most certainly does, my daughter. All places exist in Nome."

"And you have known about Nome for a very long time I suppose," Deetra said seriously, wondering why he had never mentioned Nome to her.

Starn nodded. "It was not my place to tell you of it," he said. "Nome is the seat of power for the Askan. Only an adept can open your awareness of it and only when you are ready."

Deetra thought of Malitara Tatz and how he had chided her to discover Nome. Then she thought of her father's statement that Nome was the seat of power for the Askan and for a moment she went deeply within herself, trying to grasp the possibilities.

"It is a wonderful adventure to be aware of Nome." Starn said, hearing her thoughts. "And there is no sense trying to see it all at once. It reveals itself as we are ready to grasp it."

"What did you mean that I was in danger?" Deetra asked.

"As I said, there are negative forces in Nome which have their roots elsewhere," Starn said.

"Rooted where?" Deetra asked.

Starn looked deeply once more into his daughter's eyes. He loved her. She had been the flower of his life, yet now he did not know if he could tolerate her, or the pain she was causing him.

[*141*]

Deetra saw in his gaze what her father was feeling and she was deeply moved, frightened by it. She took a step back, closed her eyes briefly and then reopened them. "The roots of this negative force you speak of," she said, "are they within me?"

Starn nodded. "Yes, my daughter. It is you that they are within."

Deetra did not answer but turned about, looking in the distance to the area of the summit from where she had travelled. She knew now what her father was trying to communicate to her. In her rejection of the Hanta consciousness, she had given power to the negative force, and she was, in a sense, yielding to it instead. She was drawing danger to herself and because Starn loved her as his child, he could not help but be in sympathy with her and was therefore endangering himself. The others he spoke of must have been enduring a similar self-torture as she was.

"I would like to go to the others," Deetra said. "Perhaps together we can strengthen each other."

Starn appeared shocked. "It is the way of the negative force," he said. "Can't you see, my daughter, that one yielding to the negative force is like those who are yielding to the same force. You cannot go to them except in forming an alliance with them. Like attracts like in the lower worlds." He paused, feeling helpless. "Daughter, the only solution is that you yield to the Hanta consciousness," Starn said.

She looked away. "I cannot," she said softly. "I wish I could, but I cannot do it."

"You must," he said determinedly.

"I cannot," she said. "I must maintain my own identity."

"But you don't understand," Starn said. "In merging you become more of yourself than ever."

Deetra studied her father. "Are you telling me that you have yielded?" she asked.

[*142*]

"No," he said, "it is not my time to yield."

"And why is that?" she asked. "Does each person have a time for yielding?"

"Yes!"

"And how can you be so sure that you will yield when you are called?"

"I know," he said. "That is why I have not yet been called. First, I have other things to attend. I must see to it that you are first cut free; that our bond is severed and our karma wiped clean."

"You are saying that your time for yielding will come following mine," Deetra said.

"Yes."

"It seems unfair that I hold you up," Deetra said.

"I am the one who incurred the debt in another lifetime," Starn said. "That is why you have the power to hold me up."

"And do you know exactly what the debt is?" Deetra asked.

"Yes."

"May I know as well?" she asked.

Starn looked down toward the ground as though ashamed. Slowly he raised his head and looked into his daughter's eyes. "I once stood in your way when you wanted to yield to the Hanta consciousness," he said softly. Tears filled his eyes. "And it is for that reason that I may not yield until you do so in this life."

Deetra watched as the tears dripped down her father's face. She wanted to reach out to him; to comfort him, but she knew that to do so would be futile. She could not surrender herself to the Hanta consciousness for her father's sake. She had to do it for herself if she was to do it at all.

"Where will you go from here?" she asked.

Starn looked deeply into his daughter's face. "I will climb to the summit," he said, "and wait there."

Deetra lowered her eyes and slowly turned away. She

[*143*]

headed down the trail toward Moonwalk.

But she did not get far.

A short distance down the path she saw two figures moving in and around the trees and bushes off the trail to the left. She called to them but there was no answer. "Please wait!" she called again. "It is Deetra, please wait!"

The figures, two men, stopped and turned about, looking after her, waving.

Deetra started toward them, then quickly caught herself. She did not recognize the figures, although they seemed to recognize her. They were not from her village. Suddenly she recalled how Starn had cautioned her and for some unseen reason she felt the memory of that warning now. She quickly turned about and hurried back to the trail, starting to return to the summit.

They came running toward her, catching her by the arms and backed her up against a tree.

"You called us and then run away," the one said, gruffly. His eyes were cold and feelingless and his facial features rigid. "That's not very hospitable," the other said. "Now where are you going?"

"My father awaits me on the summit," Deetra said, trying to appear calm, yet she knew that she was not successful. Her voice caught in a tremor.

"You wouldn't want to run from us now, would you?" the first one asked.

"Leave her be, Jason," the other said, pulling his arms from the girl. "We have no need to hurt her." Then he turned and moved his face just inches from hers. "Do we?" he said, spitting the words from between his teeth.

Deetra flattened herself against the tree to avoid the spray of saliva but did not speak. Whoever these men were, they were not anyone she knew or had seen, nor did she feel it likely that they were anyone Starn knew. "Who are you?" she asked, trying to appear unafraid.

The one who had been speaking grinned at her. "This

is Jason," he said in gruff accent, "and my name's Torrance. We live in these mountains. We was going home when you called us, and nice it was of you to do so."

"I thought you were someone else," Deetra said, moving a few inches from the tree and standing in a more natural position.

"And who did ya think we was?" Torrance asked, wiping his mouth with his hand.

"Someone from my village perhaps," Deetra said.

"What village?" Jason asked.

"At the foot of the mountain, near the forest," Deetra said.

"There's no village near here," Torrance said. "This is our land and you're trespassing on it."

Deetra was too astounded to speak. What were these men saying. It was not their mountain, nor anyone's mountain. It was simply the mountain and belonged to whoever chose to go there.

"Where was you goin'?" Jason asked, pointing toward the summit.

"To meet my father," Deetra said.

"He's not up there," Jason said, slapping his hand on his trousers. "There's no one up there."

"But he is," Deetra said. "I left him a few moments ago."

"Then why are you goin' back?" Torrance asked.

"Because I want to," Deetra said, lowering her eyes. What was happening? These men were little more than animals. They were questioning her, threatening her in a sense, and for no reason.

"She wants to," Jason mimicked, looking at Torrance. "Now do you think we ought to let her do that?" Then he turned to Deetra and poked her in the stomach with his finger. "Why did ya want to?" he asked.

Deetra looked at the man in the eyes. Was she so out of control that she had yielded control of this moment of her life to these men? Was she controlled by their state of consciousness? She did not have to be. She was Askan!

"Do you know who I am?" Deetra asked.

"You're a proud talking little woman," Jason said, then he grinned. "Of course we know who ya are. You're the Lady Deetra and you're here wandering the mountainside for the same reason we are."

"I don't understand you," Deetra said.

"Ya don't now," Jason said thoughtfully, narrowing his eyes. "Well I think ya do."

"Leave her alone," Torrance cut in. "She doesn't recognize us."

Deetra turned to Torrance and looked hard at the disheveled man. "No, I don't know you," she said. "But I have the feeling I should."

"Exactly right," Jason said, leaning his body toward her again. "You should indeed."

"Please tell me who you are," Deetra said.

"We told you our names," Jason said.

"Yes, but who are you to me?" Deetra asked.

Torrance laughed, "Well that we can't tell."

"You are brothers?" Deetra asked.

The two men looked at Deetra, then at each other and burst out laughing again. They laughed so hard they doubled over as though out of control. Deetra backed away from them but was caught when Jason grabbed her arm.

"You don't get away that easy, little woman," Jason said.

"Now take it easy, brother," Torrance said.

Jason grinned at the word brother.

"We don't need to hurt her," Torrance said again.

Jason let go of Deetra's arm. "You say you tell the truth," he said to her "Well, if that's so, will you promise not to run away?"

Deetra rubbed her arm where Jason had held her. A deep red mark smarted her flesh to prove what seemed unreal to be actually happening, then she looked at Jason. His expression appeared hard and calloused. There was little doubt that next time he would hurt her if she tried to escape. "I promise," she said.

"Good," he said, nodding that he was satisfied.

Torrance pulled Jason aside, but Deetra could hear what he was saying. "She doesn't recognize us," Torrance was saying, "what will we do if she never does?"

"She will," Jason answered.

"But suppose she don't?" Jason said.

"We could help her," Torrance said.

"No," Jason said. "Why should we? It's because of her that we're like this anyway. If she dies, she dies!"

Torrance bumped Jason on the arm and purposely pushed him slightly. "You're stupid, Jason!" he snapped angrily. "If she dies so will we."

Jason stood looking at Torrance in disbelief, shaking his head. "Talk about being dumb," he said, "you're the dumb one!"

"What do ya mean?"

"We're goin' to die anyway," Jason said. "It doesn't matter if she recognizes us or don't recognize us. Just as soon as the old man comes off the summit we're goin' to die."

"What old man?" Deetra called out from behind them.

The two men turned about and saw that she had been listening. Jason reached for her angrily but Torrance held him back.

"As soon as what old man comes from the summit?" Deetra asked again.

"As soon as THE old man comes," Jason shot back.

"Who is that?" Deetra asked again, unable to draw any mental imagery from the two men.

"She don't know," Torrance said.

"Then why tell her?" Jason said.

"Because you said it didn't make any difference,"

Deetra said quickly.

The two men looked at one another. "She's smart," Jason said.

"Maybe too smart," Torrance said.

"Does it matter?" Deetra shouted. "Please tell me about the old man who will come down from the summit."

"Will you help us?" Torrance asked.

"She can't help us," Jason interrupted.

"If I can, I will," Deetra said. "I promise that if I can help, I will, but you must tell me."

"Tell her," Torrance said, nudging him.

"You tell her," Jason said.

"Please, will one of you tell me," Deetra said urgently.

"Okay," Torrance said, looking first at her, then Jason, then toward the summit and back to Deetra again. "Every hundred years the old man comes down from the summit," Torrance said, holding his gaze firmly on Deetra. "And when he does everything which exists becomes non-existent and everything that is non-existent suddenly exists." He paused, his gaze searching her face. "That's how it happens," he said. "We that is living suddenly dies and them that was dead rises up from it."

Deetra stared at the man in disbelief. Could it be that he was referring to the ancient form of Hanta coming down from the summit to cause havoc in the world of matter? Was he referring to Awakening Day, the hundred year celebration of the renewal of the Hanta consciousness? "It is over," Deetra said softly. "The time that you fear is over."

"What's she saying?" Jason asked.

Torrance shook his head without shifting his eyes from Deetra. "What are you sayin'?" he asked her.

"I was there," Deetra said. "Awakening Day celebrations were held in our village three years ago."

"She's crazy!" Jason yelled.

Deetra did not know what to say and remained silent.

"What celebrations you talking about?" Torrance

asked. "And what village?"

"I can only tell you what I know from my experience," Deetra said, gradually becoming aware that these men, although they appeared to be of her dimension had to be from another. "I come from the village at the foot of the mountain. Three years ago we held Awakening Day celebrations and the old man you speak of, the Hanta, came down from the mountain just as you said." Deetra hesitated, watching the effect of her explanation on the two men. They seemed to disbelieve her. "It happened three years ago," she said again.

"Couldn't have," Jason said, his eyes narrowing into thin slits, squinting at her. "We've been watching for the old man and he never came down."

"Then perhaps you missed seeing him," Deetra said.

"Impossible," Torrance said.

"Hear that?" Jason said to Deetra. "It was impossible to miss him."

"And why is that?" Deetra asked.

"Because we waited by the trail," Torrance said. "We never leave the trail."

"But that's not true," Deetra said, "when I first saw you both, you had your backs to the trail, walking away."

"That's different," Jason said.

"Why?"

"Me and Torrance saw you coming. We only wondered if you would recognize us without us coming after you first. And you did!" Jason said.

"But I didn't," Deetra said, puzzled.

"That's right, she didn't," Torrance agreed.

"But she did!" Jason insisted. "She did for a second or else she wouldn't have called us."

"I believed you to be from our village," Deetra said.

"Did you now?" Jason said, his eyes narrowed again.

"Yes."

"Well, you take a good long look at me," Jason said,

pushing his face close to hers, noses barely touching. "Look at me and tell me you don't know me."

Deetra did not answer but looked into the face a few inches from her own. Nothing seemed familiar in that face. The features were scarred and coarse and the expression slovenly and angry. She knew no one who even faintly resembled this man, but she stared at him for what seemed a very long time, his pinched face inches from her own. Then, gradually, she saw something that she had not seen. There was an expression in the eyes which reminded her of something, not someone but something.

Jason grinned as he watched a glimmer of recognition flicker in her eyes. "She sees me," Jason said excitedly. "She sees me! Look at her,Torrance. She sees me!"

Deetra lowered her eyes, uncertain.

Jason grabbed her chin with his hand and squeezed it tightly. "Don't you look away from me," he snarled. "I've waited a long time for you to recognize me."

"But I don't," Deetra said, hesitating, looking deeply into his eyes once more. Then once again she saw something in them that she recognized. Whatever it was, was trying to communicate with her.

The thing had a life force which seemed distinctly individual, apart from Jason's physical entity. It seemed to reach out to her, begging her to give a part of herself to it. "What is it?" she asked softly, looking into Jason's eyes. "Who are you?"

"She still doesn't know!" Torrance yelled, knocking Jason on the shoulder with his fist.

Jason turned to him angrily. "Then you try," he snapped, stepping out of the way.

Deetra did not try to move.

Torrance slid in front of her where Jason had been shifting his large, overweight body back and forth in front of her, then stooped slightly so that she could look him directly in the eyes. "Now what do you see?" he said to her.

[*150*]

Deetra looked into the round, ugly face and saw that although it was sloven and lustful, it was also a kind face. She wanted to say something pleasant to it, but she caught the impulse and suppressed it. She looked away for a moment, wondering at her predicament. Why was she confronted by these two and why had she been so out of tune with herself that she could not read into their minds and understand who they were?

"She's not even trying," Jason yelled from behind Torrance. "She's not even paying any attention to you."

Deetra quickly looked at Torrance whose expression remained kindly yet stern, and something in it reminded her of Sarpent. It was a fleeting recognition and just as quickly as she perceived the Chief Elder, she dismissed the perception.

She looked again into Torrance's eyes.

"Tell what you see," Jason snapped nearby.

A sudden panic gripped at Deetra. She did not know what to say. It was not what she saw that held her. It was what she did not see. She saw nothing. Her mind churned up images of herself and chewed on them. She was talking to herself inwardly, arguing with herself. It was as though she was on the brink of going to war with herself.

What was happening?

She tried to shut out the chatter; to listen to it without recognition of the words being said, and somewhere, deep within the recesses of her mental faculty, she heard a thin voice pleading for her attention.

"Who are you?" her mind asked.

The voice answered, but it was a thin voice without distinction. It sounded like the sound of HU, only it was the HU that seemed to be trying to verbalize something.

That was it!

The sound HUuuuu was the voice and it contained the message she was trying to hear. She strained to listen, to know what it was, what *it* was saying, but her attention faltered. She was being drawn in two directions at once—the HU and the gruff sounds made by the two men with her.

"Damn it, Torrance, she's trying to get away from us," Jason said.

"She can't get away," Torrance said, still staring at Deetra. "The only way she could get away from us is if we weren't here."

"Well, you just watch her," Jason said suspiciously. "I don't want her getting away from us until she recognizes who we are."

"Maybe she's about to do that," Torrance said, looking at Deetra.

Deetra was distracted by the men but also nourished by them. At first she was ashamed to admit it to herself, but as they tore at her to recognize them, she was becoming aware of other things.

Mostly she was aware of the bani or sound current in a way she had never recognized. The HU, she knew, was the voice of the Supreme One, the SUGMAD, but until now she never considered that the voice communicated anything but the sound itself. The voice was trying to tell her something.

Something!

That was it!

Some-thing!

She remembered how when she had looked into Jason's eyes she had seen the presence of *some-thing* and how the thing seemed alive, an entity trying to communicate with her. She remembered, too, how Jason had been excited by her recognition of the *thing;* how he felt that she was on the verge of recognizing him.

Then the spell was broken and she lost her concentration.

What had happened?

Deetra tried to recall every little detail of what had transpired to make her lose her concentration. She had been

[*152*]

calling out to *it*, asking *it* to identify *itself* when Torrance had knocked Jason out of the way. If he had left her one more minute she might have known. Why did he interrupt at that particular moment?

"She's trying to get away from us again," Jason snapped, pushing Torrance out of the way. Then he pushed Deetra next to the tree. "Now listen to me, little lady," he said angrily, "until you recognize us, you aren't going to get away from us. Now that means you're not going to be free until then. Do you understand what I'm saying?"

Deetra nodded slowly, thoughtfully. "Why is it so important to you," she asked, "to either of you?" She looked from face to face.

"Tell her," Torrance said. "I think we ought to tell her."

Jason turned angrily to Torrance. "Don't you think I'd like to do that," he said, "but what happens when we do? I'll tell you what happens. She's free but we're still imprisoned by her. She has to discover our identity for herself!"

Torrance motioned Jason over to him and whispered something. Jason whispered back and the two of them continued conversing in this way so that Deetra could not hear what they were saying. It was some minutes before they turned to face her again. Jason was smiling triumphantly.

"We're goin' to take a walk," Torrance said lightly. "Jason's goin' to lead, you follow and I'll take up the rear."

"Where are we going?" Deetra asked.

"Just around the mountain," Torrance said. "It's nothing to worry yourself about."

"But I've heard that some of those from my village are in difficult straits and may need assistance," Deetra said, feeling foolish that she had spoken.

"Now if that don't beat all," Jason said. "I'd say you're in a difficult strait yourself. How do you figure you're goin' to help someone else?"

Deetra did not answer. It had been a stupid remark for

her to make. Her father had said that to her when first she remarked that she wanted to assist the others who were headed for Moonwalk. He had known. That was why he had gone to the summit instead. Deetra knew as well, but she did not wish to return to the summit. Only once had she thought of returning and that was to run to the safety of her father's arms when the two men had chased after her. But no, she did not yet wish to return to the summit, although she knew that the time would eventually come.

Jason gave her a push and took the lead, telling her and Torrance to stay close behind. Then he hurried off.

Deetra thought of how strange it was that she was in this predicament. To begin with, no one or no thing could keep her prisoner if only she were to call on the Hanta consciousness for assistance, but she couldn't do it. To call for help would be asking for the power's protection and in so doing she would become the power *itself*. She would yield to *it,* become *it,* or protection could not be granted. No, if she were to free herself from Jason and Torrance, she would have to do as they asked. She would have to recognize them.

But she had no idea how to begin.

"May we just stop and talk for a moment," Deetra called to Jason in the lead.

Jason did not answer but kept the hurried pace in front of them. Torrance gave her gentle pushes from the rear to keep her moving swiftly. As they walked, Deetra thought of the journey to the summit with Malitara Tatz, recalling how he had disappeared, leaving her to meet the faces peering down at her from the summit. She recalled how they had treated her, baiting her to draw her to them and how she had recognized them to be aspects of herself, aberrated aspects at that. Were these men similar entities? Were they urges of herself, aspects of her nature?

Suddenly Jason came to a stop, motioning that she sit on a large rock in the center of a clearing of trees. "Sit," he commanded "and wait there! We have a surprise for you."

Deetra did as she was told, watching as they disappeared into the bushes. A moment later Torrance returned holding a young man by the arm.

It was Rian, the scribe.

Deetra jumped from her seat and started toward them.

"Stay back," Torrance said, motioning with his free hand for her to stop. "Don't come any closer." Then he hurried Rian back into the bushes. A moment later Jason returned holding an older man by the arm.

It was Sarpent the Chief Elder and he looked directly at Deetra.

Deetra was too astounded to speak.

"Stay where ya are," Jason snapped, "you come a step closer and we're all in trouble. Now go sit down on that rock where I told you to stay," he said.

Deetra stared at the Chief Elder, hoping for some sign but he gave none. His expression was stern and sober and his mind was still. No thoughts reached out to her.

"Sit down," Jason commanded again.

As though in a dream, Deetra moved backward to the rock and seated herself, watching as Jason escorted Sarpent away. She did not try to speak with him.

Shortly both Jason and Torrance returned to the clearing, looking at Deetra. Both shook their heads. "She does not help matters any," Torrance said. "She does not try to recognize us."

"Then let's dispose of her," Jason said. "Let's just dump her. I'm tired of fooling with her and it looks like we're going to die anyway."

Deetra easily heard what the men were saying and she wanted to jump from her seat to change the verdict they were passing on her, but she couldn't. Something within her would not budge. It was as though a sudden weight had been fastened to her inwardly. She could not think, or feel and even the inner sound current seemed silent.

How could that be?

She had no answer. Her inner being was frozen in a state of inertia.

"I say, let's get rid of her," Jason said again.

Torrance did not answer, but Deetra watched as his head nodded up and down in agreement.

"You want to do it or do you want me to do it?" Jason asked.

"You do it," Torrance said.

Deetra was completely still, watching as Jason took out a knife and raised it in some sort of ritual, slowly coming toward her. At first she remained without feeling and then a knot formed at the back of her throat and in the pit of her stomach. She watched the man coming toward her and she saw that as he moved he was being transformed with each step. It was Rian. It was Sarpent. It was Tolar. It was Sonar. It was Liether. It was Starn. It was Kara. It was Malitara Tatz. It was Ramus-i-Rabriz ... It was Ian!

She looked deeply into her husband's eyes as he approached, and there she saw not only an image of herself but of all those who had touched her life and added meaning to it. As herself, she was Ian ... She was Rian ... She was Starn ... She was Sarpent ... She was Tolar ... She was Sonar ... She was Liether ... She was Kara ... She was Malitara Tatz ... She was Ramus-i-Rabriz. And then in reverse again she was the temple master Ramus-i-Rabriz. She was Malitara Tatz, the old messenger. She was Kara, the adept. She was Liether, the bodyless one. She was Sonar, the physician. She was Tolar, the student. She was Sarpent, the Chief Elder. She was her father, Starn. She was Rian, the scribe. She was Ian, the Hanta!

She was the consciousness of *all*, the Hanta consciousness, *THE Consciousness*, and here in Nome she was empowered by *it*. She rose to her feet to meet eye to eye with Jason with knife raised above his head and, looking into him, she saw that he too was herself. He was the corrupted side of the positive polarity, the ego, and in his desire to be recognized he had been consumed by pride and anger. He symbolized the last of the mind passions to yield and Torrance was his lesser brother. She did not fear them now but blessed them in the name of the Hanta. Then she turned her back upon them. It was the last she saw of Jason and Torrance.

Ahead of her was Ian calling from the summit. He called to her and she ran to him, arms outstretched.

When at last they reunited, Deetra was overjoyed to learn that they remained individual beings sharing the Hanta consciousness.

They were the power!

They were the glory!

They were the love!

They were the beingness of ALL!

They were FREE!

Their union was the ultimate, yet IT was only the beginning!